Kissed By The Gods

Kissed By The Gods

Gerald James Jackson

S.P.I.
BOOKS
A Division of Shapolsky Publishers

Kissed By The Gods

S.P.I. BOOKS
A division of Shapolsky Publishers, Inc.

ISBN 1-56171-359-7

For any additional information, contact:

S.P.I. BOOKS/Shapolsky Publishers, Inc.
136 West 22nd Street
New York, NY 10011
212/633-2022 / • FAX 212/633-2123

Manufactured in Canada

10 9 8 7 6 5 4 3 2 1

This book is
dedicated to
Richard G. Jackson
and
Glenn E. Jackson

Prologue

The East River curved like a serpent around the edge of upper Manhattan, separating it from its lesser sister, the Bronx. On this bright September morning, the river lost its sinister look as it carried the last tourists of summer on the Day Line Cruise around the wonder of Manhattan Island. From the vantage point of her Eastside penthouse, Cassandra Collins gazed down at the river below and imagined what Peter Stuyvesant would think of little New Amsterdam today. With its millions of inhabitants working and living in tall glass and cement buildings, it must seem light years removed from the small farms and villages of his day. She wondered if it would still be standing one hundred years from now.

Crossing the large room, its parquet floors covered with antique oriental carpets, Cassandra paused in front of the fireplace to gather some incense from an onyx box on the mantle. As she glanced at her reflection in the mirror that hung about the intricately carved mantlepiece, she thought how right the sharp, young reporter from *The New York Times Magazine* was to liken her deep blue eyes, auburn hair, and porcelain complexion to the young Maureen O'Hara. The resemblance, once pointed out, seemed uncanny.

The cut glass crystals hanging inside the open windows broke the sunlight into hundreds of brilliant rainbows that danced merrily throughout the apartment. It seemed ironic how these perfect spectrums of color and light contrasted with the imperfect lives of the men and women she counseled as a clairvoyant in this room for the last fourteen years. As the morning sun poured over her body, she deeply inhaled the smoke from her Dunhill cigarette, promising herself that she would free herself of this last nasty habit as soon as she was settled in her new home in the Carolinas. She had already beaten coffee and sugar in her new health regime, but she wasn't going to even try kicking tobacco until her life was relatively calm.

Cassandra looked around the room at all the boxes and packing crates. She felt happy inside, despite the mess lying all around. She could never bring herself to call this apartment home and although it had appeared in *Town and Country* and *Architectural Digest*, she thought it had never looked better than it did right now. The truth of the matter was, although she dearly loved the little world she had created from another time and place, an eighteenth century salon, she never felt at home in the impersonal steel and glass high rise which encased it and, as she oftentimes felt, her soul.

Cassandra pushed several boxes out of the way to make room for her morning ritual. She lit a candle for serenity and burned a cube of incense for purification. Drawing a deep breath, she cleared her lungs and began her yoga sun salutes with a prayer, asking to be a worthy steward of her psychic gifts. After completing her yoga postures and stretches, she sat upright in her favorite blue silk chair for her morning meditation. Ever since she had lived in this apartment she had begun each morning this way, and movers or not, she saw no reason to interrupt her routine.

Feeling totally relaxed after her half hour meditation, Cassandra knew intuitively the movers would be delayed in a traffic snarl coming into Manhattan over the 59th Street Bridge. She seized the opportunity to have one long last look at the view that was the envy of all her friends; savoring it and remembering every detail with an intensity usually reserved for the face of a perfect lover you somehow knew you would never see again. Lighting a cigarette, Cassandra let the smoke slowly fill her lungs and continued staring through the window at what appeared to be the orderly world below. From high above the noise and the filth, it all seemed so beautiful, but on the street it was the antithesis of a Clairol commercial, the closer you looked or sniffed, the fouler it became.

Cassandra had no doubts about the Exodus. Even though her friends thought her mad to leave New York, Cassandra wanted out. Out of the city, out of the pressure, out of the unreal chrysalis she had created. She felt deep inside life held something more than lunches at the Russian Tea Room, box seats at the Metropolitan Opera, and relationships with men who were afraid of loving a real, flesh and blood woman; men who seemed cardboard figures of cold, economic fact and mechanical lust. She wanted to share her life with one true male who was willing and able to explore his mind, body, and soul with her and intermingle their essences to create a different, richer, more sublime reality than either could attain alone.

Her friends asked questions: "Darling, what will you do, wherever are you moving? How will you spend your time? You really must be kidding to give up all you have attained ln New York, aren't you?" Cassandra calmly replied: "You know I will miss my friends, but 1 will be fine, doing my counseling, lecturing, and writing. I just want to escape from the mad vibrations of New York and the city lights. It is as simple as that." She loved watching her friends shake their heads in dismay, believing Manhattan to be Mount Olympus, the top of the world. She felt with every atom of her being there just had to be a better way to live, and in her heart she believed that she would find it.

Material things no longer mattered to Cassandra. What mattered to her now was living a life filled with meaning, with peace and contentment. She had up until this point in her life known very little serenity, except for the quiet moments she stole in meditation and the satisfaction of her work. Her personal life had been a soap opera and she was determined to change all that. The real estate agent who sold Cassandra her North Carolina estate had lined up ten new clients for her clairvoyant counseling sessions and her new publicist had booked her on the Sea Princess for a speaking engagement on a week long Carribean cruise. Things could not appear brighter, except for the inner gnawing of a woman desiring her mate.

Cassandra made up her mind to close the door on her past. Shedding Philip had been as easy as taking a bath, it left only a ring of scum around the tub. Beautiful Bobby had been taken from her like the dawn takes an unreal dream, leaving only a vague, haunting memory. Only Peter hadn't left her consciousness, and Cassandra resigned herself to the fact that he would always remain there, lurking beneath her calm exterior, like an eel under the surface of a crystal lake, ready at a moment's notice to steal around her heart, strangling her, pulling her down into the black pit of emotional despair. She was hoping her new life in the Carolinas would somehow enable her to release him from her life forever, something that New York never allowed. She was a fighter, if nothing else, and she would not let her feeling keep her from moving on. She would resolve it someday, but for now she had to forget him.

Her reverie was suddenly interrupted by the noisy intercom. The unearthly buzz rang through the apartment, signaling that the moving men were downstairs, the spell was broken. Cassandra hastily put out the cigarette and answered the buzzer.

"Yes."

"Miss Collins, the moving men are here. Shall I let them up?"

"That will be fine, Samuel, thank you."

She went over to the huge oak door in the foyer and unlocked it. Faced with the reality of last minute packing, Cassandra walked to the window for the last time and gently removed her crystals from the window. Sitting down on the long, blue velvet sofa, she carefully wrapped each one in tissue paper. Looking around the room at all the boxes was an exhilarating experience for her. She was excited about the move and the attendant promise it held for her. The movers would strip the apartment of everything except the three small boxes at her feet which she would take with her in her silver-blue Mercedes sports coupe on the twelve-hour drive to her new home and new-found freedom.

They were her three treasure chests. The first held her diaries and writings, the second held her fabulous collection of jewels, and the third held her most precious souvenirs: her picture from the cover of *People Magazine*, the Scavullo portrait of her taken for *Vogue* and the crystals collected on her many trips around the world. The lid of the last box was the only one to remain open, for Cassandra had one last memento to pack in her sacred cache, the silver Tiffany baby cup given to her on the day of her Christening. It was inscribed,

"To My Beloved Daughter, Cassandra,
MAY YOUR LIFE BE KISSED BY THE GODS
Your Loving Father,
Arthur Edward Collins, 11-12-1949."

In her last symbolic act before leaving the apartment, she picked up the baby cup and kissed it, then wrapped it and packed it securely away. Not unlike the Greek Fates, she finished her life in New York by measuring the adhesive tape, cutting it, and finally, sealing the last box.

BOOK ONE

Chapter One

Bad news never waits until morning.

With a sense of foreboding Sarah Cullen Collins answered the telephone in her dark Greenwich Village townhouse. The loud ringing contrasted sharply to the stillness of the quiet December night. As she reached over to the nightstand to turn on a light and find her bifocals, those damn glasses she swore she would never become dependent upon, she wondered who could be calling in the middle of the night on her private line.

"Yes, who is it?"

"Father Flaherty, Ma'am. May I speak to Mrs. Collins, please."

"This is she." As she spoke, she felt as if the top of her head was going to come off. She must remember to take a pressure pill before she went back to sleep.

"Mrs. Collins, I'm sorry to inform you there has been a terrible car accident. Your son is critically injured and his wife, I'm afraid, didn't make it."

"My God." Sarah went into shock.

"Your son is begging for you to come.

I have administered the last rites."

"Thank you, Father. Where is he?"

"Mercy Hospital in Rockville Centre."

"I'll be there as soon as I can get a car."

"Would you like me to wait for you?" the kind Irish priest asked her.

"No thank you, Father. I'll be fine alone."

Although she was a very spiritual woman, Sarah had an innate dislike for the men of the cloth. In her mind she associated them with the black birds that hovered about the funeral corteges she remembered from her early childhood in England. Only five years before, a priest brought her the news of her sons, Erick and John, dying on the beaches of Normandy during the Allied invasion of Europe, and now her only surviving son lay critically injured in a hospital. Despite her own pain and anxiety, all Sarah could think about were her three grandchildren, baby Cassandra, barely six weeks old, and the. twins, Tom and Ryan, seven years old.

As she hurriedly dressed, her mind drifted back to a scene two weeks earlier, at her son's large colonial home in Garden City. The house was decorated for a double celebration, the christening of his first daughter and the twins' seventh birthday. Everyone had been so happy, and now, everything had changed. Her mind flashed to her daughter-in-law, Norah, who was so beautiful and alive. You would never believe she had just given birth to an eight pound baby, and now she was in some hospital morgue, dead.

Sarah grabbed her silver rosary beads and began praying,

"Hail Mary, full of grace, the Lord is with thee . . ." As she waited impatiently for the limousine to arrive, she thought to herself, bad news never waits.

Chapter Two

The big country kitchen of the Collins' Long Island estate had the unmistakable touch of a grandmother's love. From the embroidered tablecloth to the carefully folded chequered napkins, everything was a welcome sign to sit down for a cup of freshly brewed tea and a slice of hot, homebaked Irish soda bread with fresh cream and homemade jam. The big copper kettle was constantly boiling for the friends and family of Sarah Cullen Collins, who spent the majority of her day in this room taking care of the children's needs and supervising the Collins household. Sarah was a tall woman with bright blue eyes, her beautiful white hair pulled back into a chignon. Dressing always in shades of blue, possessed of unlimited patience and grace, and having the answers to all the questions a child could possibly ask, Cassandra found it easy to pretend that her grandmother was the real life Blue Fairy from *Pinnochio.* Sarah was her paternal grandmother, the only parent Cassandra had ever known, her parents having been killed four weeks after her birth.

When confronted by life's ups and downs, Sarah prayed for a solution, and then acted upon it without hesitation; and when presented with three orphaned children at the ripe age of 66, she set herself into action once again, claiming it was in her stars as a Leo, Leo being the sign of royalty, and in her Irish blood, Ireland being the land of deposed kings and queens. "Her Majesty," as she was referred to behind her back took over her son's household the day after he and his wife were buried, and lay down the law with complete authority to her twin grandsons and household staff. It was clear in everyone's mind what was expected of them, no questions asked, thank you very much. No one dared cross Sarah's path or thwart her will. Compared to her, Rose Kennedy was a pussycat, but no one was more generous or compassionate than she.

Fate had thrown Sarah several bad curves in her life, but she never once complained, believing adversity built character, and Divine Providence had everything under control. The main emotion seen on her face was serenity, which came from her belief in the goodness of life, that every bad thing along the way also contained the seed of an equivalent good. Being an only child, Sarah nurtured in her heart the idea of someday being the matriarch of a great dynasty, but Fate seemed to rob her of her dream.

Her husband died an early death from cirrhosis of the liver brought on by his incipient alcoholism. She was able to bear only three sons, having had a hysterectomy to save her life after the birth of her third, and least favorite son, Arthur, who turned out to have the same easy charm as his father, along with his same weakness for whiskey, women, and gambling. The first two sons were killed on the beaches of Normandy during the Allied attach on D-Day, before they had the chance to marry and bring new life into the Collins family, and now Arthur was dead, leaving her with three orphans. Sarah looked upon her grandchildren as the opportunity to have her dream reach fulfillment. The day after Arthur's funeral, Sarah Collins rented out her Greenwich Village townhouse, and left behind her wonderful life in New York to take care of her three young wards, bringing with her only her clothes, china, silver and books.

Sarah was quite different from the other wealthy women of her day, and it was no wonder with the upbringing she had had. Her mother, Esther Cullen, was a gifted psychic who was able to pierce the veil that separated the world of the seen from the unseen. Sarah was close to her mother and looked up to her with a devotion one usually saw reserved for saints. Esther's deep aquamarine eyes seemed to read your thoughts and pierce your soul.

Esther Cullen was twenty-three years old, pregnant, and unmarried when she left Ireland to seek her fortune in London. The society in which Esther found herself was exciting; the repression of the Victorian Era was disappearing to make way for a freer and more permissive society. Because of her psychic gifts, she was welcome in the best homes. Only one other psychic, Count Louis Hamon, had a bigger following, and when he was forced by a romantic scandal to flee London, Esther gratefully "inherited" his high society clientele and became the toast of the town, making a good living for her newly born daughter, Sarah, and herself.

However busy or pushed she was, she never failed to put her daughter's welfare first and was a wonderful and loving mother. She exposed her to the best that London had to offer in the way of education, beauty and culture. In the evenings, Sarah sat spellbound, listening to her mother read from the great writers of the day in a soothing, musical voice with an endearing Irish brogue.

In some ways, Sarah was sheltered; she spent her days with the teaching sisters of St. Mary's Academy for Girls, but Esther tried to make up for it by introducing her to friends from the worlds of journalism, politics and theater. When they were alone, they retired into the drawing room of their spacious flat in London's prestigious Marble Arch and had tea and pudding, discussing the daily events of their own lives, and the world. Sarah learned about politics, the economy, and business. Esther believed a young lady should know everything about the world, because one day she might have to support herself, as she had had to do. Sarah accepted the education with an eagerness indicating her sharp mind.

It was a usual occurrence for Sarah to ask her mother's advice on every problem she encountered, and although Esther believed adversity built character, she had a weak spot where her own daughter was concerned. Unwittingly, she encouraged an unnatural dependency, making the familiar parental mistake of trying to help one's child in every way possible. Esther rationalized this behavior by stating, "Where would Jesus be if it weren't for Mary?"

The only gap in Sarah's prolific education was knowledge of her father. He was never mentioned except to say he was a great man and, when she was of age, she would be told all about him. The fact remained: Sarah never learned his identity.

Rivers and lives have a great deal in common for just when you are sure of the direction they are flowing, an unexpected turn appears and they change courses completely. When Sarah was sixteen years old, her life took such a turn.

One evening, after an early dinner of stuffed pheasant, potatoes, gravy, and homebaked French bread, Esther took her daughter aside.

"Sarah, I've had a very strong premonition which I must share with you."

"Yes, Mother. What is it?"

"I dreamed you will be leaving London to go across the waters to America. There you will meet a man, handsome as the devil with bright red hair to match. He is charming, but not to be trusted."

"I'm not planning to leave home, Mother," Sarah protested. "And, besides, I don't even know any men my age."

"Listen carefully, Sarah. Sometimes life is not what we plan. If you marry this man, you will become wealthy and bear him three children, but you will be very lonely." Esther looked far away as if Sarah weren't present in the room.

"Why is this so, Mother? Is everything in the future written?"

"No, dear," Esther spoke slowly. "God

gives everyone a bit of free will. It is our gift, to use wisely or foolishly. We learn and grow through experience. Your personal happiness, however, lies with your choice of mate."

"I have always taken your advice, Mother, don't look so forlorn." Sarah smiled, adding, "I'll try to avoid redheads."

"I hope so." Esther touched Sarah's face lovingly. "I must be off to the theater. Good night, dear."

Esther turned and left the room. Little did Sarah realize she would never see her mother alive again, for that evening, on her way home an artery burst inside Esther's brain, killing her in minutes.

True to Esther's prophecy, Sarah emigrated to New York City shortly after her mother's death, to stay with distant cousins. Soon thereafter, she met thirty-year old Harold Collins, a tall, handsome redhaired bachelor of considerable charm and fortune. After a whirlwind courtship, they married and Sarah promptly bore him three fine sons in four years. Harold's considerable fortune was made by burying the rich, the middle class, and the poor: everyone who could afford a funeral, wooden box, and rented carriage. His failing to reform his bachelor habits after marriage was a source of considerable grief for Sarah.

Harold was a great socializer, incredible womanizer, and inveterate alcoholic, but he had the gift of making money. Like all good Irish women of her generation, Sarah didn't believe in divorce, leaving only murder as the unthinkable alternative. Most women believed that if the husband was a good provider and didn't beat his wife, she was lucky. Though Sarah wasn't in total agreement with the sentiment, being a realist, she didn't complain and made the marriage work.

She refused to let her husband make her life miserable, and took solace in overseeing the lives of her three sons, and investing Harold's money in lucrative real estate deals. She stood proudly to see her three sons graduating from Ivy League schools. Sarah believed women to be the backbone of the Collins family, as they had been in the Cullen family, holding it together with faith, a determination to succeed, and not letting anyone forget it.

Cassandra never tired of asking her

grandmother about the story of her childhood's growing up in London, and although Sarah never actually lied to the child, she tended to embellish the story over the years. Sarah's mother, like Cassandra, was born with the "veil", or caul, over her face, which was indicative to the superstitious Irish of the gift of second sight. Sarah always felt tainted by having been born a bastard and her late husband was convinced this was the reason for his beautiful wife's was obsession with royalty.

Esther's death left Sarah with the loss, not only of a beloved mother, but a trusted advisor. She had developed a dependency upon her psychic gift for guidance. The only time she failed to heed a warning was when she met and married Harold. She vowed after the marriage she would never again dismiss spiritual advice. From the time she arrived in New York she was unable to find any psychic, astrologer, or medium she trusted. Most turned out to be fakes, liars, crazy, or a combination of all three, but Sarah still sought them out.

One day, while she was sitting in the beauty parlor, Sarah overheard a conversation about a neighborhood gypsy woman who lived on Christopher Street in the heart of Greenwich Village. Sarah made it her business to learn the woman's name and make an appointment the same day.

Sarah went to the large apartment building on the corner of Waverly and Christopher. She looked up Mrs. Veilo's name on the apartment directory and rang her on the intercom. A woman's voice answered and, when Sarah identified herself, she was buzzed in. Sarah found the apartment and rang the doorbell. After a few moments, she heard a muffled voice call out, "Yes, I'll be right there." After another minute or so, the door opened and an old Rumanian woman, apparently in her late seventies, suffering from arthritis and partially blinded by cataracts, welcomed her inside.

"Come inside, my dear. I am Mrs. Veilo," the old woman smiled. "I am sorry it took so long to answer the door, but I was on the telephone when you arrived."

"Good to meet you, Mrs. Veilo. I am Sarah Cullen Collins." Sarah extended her aristocratic, gloved hand and the old gypsy warmly shook hands.

As Sarah entered the apartment she was immediately reminded of her own childhood in England. The apartment, although very old, and looking in need of a good cleaning, was furnished with heavy Victorian furniture, upholstered in burgundy velvet which showed a great deal of wear.

"Would you like to join me in some tea?" Mrs. Veilo asked, as she poured herself a cup from a beautiful old china tea pot.

"No, thank you. I am rather anxious to have my reading. I have heard so many fine things about you."

Mrs. Veilo smiled, "I hope you will not be disappointed." She asked Sarah to give her a piece of jewelry or a personal object to hold while she made her attunement. Sarah unclasped her mother's Italian cameo pin and placed it on the table. Holding the brooch, Mrs. Veilo closed her eyes and took several deep breaths. After two or three minutes a voice, higher pitched and distinctly different from the old woman's, began to emerge from deep in her throat. Sarah was a little startled at first, but she was mesmerized by what the voice had to say. It indicated she had immigrated to New York from London and had married a red-haired alcoholic. It went on to say she had three sons, and proceeded to describe each one in detail. The voice recounted Sarah's life until that point and made several predictions for the future, one of which Sarah couldn't understand. The puzzling prediction concerned a little girl who possessed the same gifts as Sarah's mother and who would be reared by her.

Almost thirty years later, when her only granddaughter, Cassandra, was born with the veil, Mrs. Veilo's curious prophecy came to pass. Although not the last bit psychic herself, Sarah fully intended to cultivate her grandchild's gift, all the while remembering her own mother's saying, "God works through people, as well as angels." And if the world ever needed help, it was in the last half of the twentieth century, with two world wars behind it and an uncertain future ahead.

Chapter Three

Little Cassandra loved her grandmother more than anyone else, and Sarah doted on her little angel more than the children she bore from her own loins. Sarah made certain Cassandra never felt like an orphan with her around. One day, Cassandra asked, "Grandmother, are you always happy?"

"No one is always happy, dear, but I look at all my blessings whenever I feel blue and it always seems to cheer me up." Sarah smiled at her granddaughter. "Why do you ask?"

"Oh, I don't know. I was just wondering if life gets easier when you are all grown up?"

Sarah put her arm around the child's shoulders. "If only it did, dear, how we would all look forward to growing old." She thought to herself about the great happiness the child had brought her, even though she came to her through tragedy.

Sometimes the twins felt excluded because Sarah didn't seem to have the patience with them she had with Cassandra. Sarah felt they had the strong determination of the Collins men and she didn't want to coddle them too much, "The Lord knows the world won't when they have to make a living in it." Sarah encouraged their love of sports, and the twins did very well at all competitive sports. She thought it also good for them to have positive male influence in their lives so they would maybe escape the CIA syndrome (Catholic Irish Alcoholics) which had claimed both their father and grandfather. When they were of high school age they were properly sent off to Kent, a New England prep school, where they would be groomed for the Ivy League life they were meant to live. Cassandra was a different story. Sarah intended to shield and protect this shy child from the harsh realities of life. What she failed to realize was Cassandra wasn't simply overprotected; she didn't enjoy wasting time with little girl games, when she would rather be painting, playing the piano, or discussing the realities of life with her best friend, Sarah. Compared to her grandmother, little girls were boring and silly. Cassandra seemed born about seventy years of age, as Sarah often proclaimed.

Sarah wanted to ensure that everything was perfect for her granddaughter. Never having had a daughter of her own to fuss over. Cassandra was dressed like a porcelain doll, her clothes were those of a princess, and her room was a child's fantasy come true, including a doll castle fully furnished. The twins were treated well, but Sarah believed all boys needed were lots of love, a good education, and a firm belief in themselves. Then they could conquer the world. A woman on the other hand needed all these things and more, because in the society in which Sarah was raised, a woman also needed to marry well. Sarah was determined Cassandra would have nothing but the best, and would not suffer the fate of herself, her mother, and grandmother of unhappy memory and unhappy romance. She wanted Cassandra to be happy, but in her secret heart feared the Collins women were cursed in love.

When Cassandra was about to begin school Sarah felt it important to start her off with a psychic reading. Mrs. Veilo, the gifted medium had already gone to her appointment with the angel of death, so Cassandra received her first reading from Mrs. Veilo's daughter, Ginger, who shared her mother's gift, but who also had a Ph.D. in psychology from New York University.

Although she missed her many friends and former life in Manhattan, Sarah's duty to her family overcame any feelings of regret she might have had. Sarah made it a point to go into Manhattan every few months and see a matinee with a friend, have lunch, have her hair done, and go shopping. On these forays into the city, she went alone, leaving Cassandra with a baby-sitter . Having a reading with Ginger Veilo would be Cassandra's first visit to the city, and Sarah intended her to have a wonderful time. The child was naturally curious and loved the ride on the Long Island Railroad into Pennsylvania Station. The city was such a contrast to their quiet life on Long Island. All the noise, tall buildings, and strange people both fascinated and frightened Cassandra. Her grandmother, aware of her mixed reaction, reassured her she would come to love the city and its excitement.

Sarah arranged their appointment with Ginger for two o'clock so she would have time for lunch at the Russian Tea Room with Danny Darcello, a top New York decorator, who was one of Sarah's dearest friends. Although gay and a good twenty-five years younger than she was, Sarah always felt more at home with him than with any of her other friends. Danny had the greatest sense of humor and he always knew all the latest Manhattan gossip. He also shared Sarah's love of the supernatural, an interest few of her other friends shared. They met years before at one of Mrs. Veilo's seances. Danny helped Sarah redecorate her townhouse in the Village and they became very close friends. Although almost forty years old, Danny looked years younger. He worked out several days a week in a gym, and he always kept his skin beautifully tanned .

Danny was already waiting at their table for lunch when Sarah and Cassandra arrived. Danny was happy to see Sarah. He rose and gave her a big hug. "How's my sweetheart doing?"

Sarah glowed, "Just fine and dandy for a tough old bird. Good to see you, love. You're looking grand."

Danny looked down to see the lovely child with the braided auburn hair and tortoise shell glasses, dressed immaculately in a white pinafore. "This must be Cassandra."

"Yes, she is. My pride and joy," Sarah beamed. Cassandra was a little shy. "Say hello to your Uncle Danny, Cassandra."

Cassandra curtsied and said very softly, "Nice to meet you." Immediately, she captured Danny's heart.

"Why, sit down, young lady. I haven't seen you since your christening. Now that you've grown, you must persuade your granny to bring you into the city and we can go to the ballet and theater."

Cassandra was a little embarrassed by all the attention, but she smiled sweetly. While the grown-ups talked and caught up on all the latest gossip, Cassandra was lost in her own world. She loved the restaurant with its bright brass samovars and the Christmas decorations done up in the middle of June. Sarah ordered sandwiches and pastries, which they all enjoyed. Cassandra felt like a little princess amid all the waiters in their bright Russian outfits and although she had never before experienced anything like it, characteristically, she felt right at home.

The lunchtime flew by for all of them. Danny happened to glance down at his gold Cartier tank watch, a present from Sarah several years before, and saw it was almost one thirty. "You'd better hurry up and get a cab, otherwise you'll be late."

Sarah got up. "Danny, you're right. We've got to run." She reached over and kissed him on the cheek. "Thank you for the lovely lunch dear. I'll let you know how the reading goes later." Taking Cassandra's hand she added, "Say good-bye, dear."

Cassandra extended her hand, "Good-bye, Uncle Danny."

"Good-bye, Cassandra. Take good care of your granny."

"Don't worry, I will."

As they left Cassandra asked her grandmother if Danny was her boyfriend. Sarah laughed and told her he wasn't. "Well, I really liked him, Grandmother."

"I know he liked you, too, dear."

Outside the Tea Room, the doorman hailed them a cab and they rode to Ginger Veilo's apartment on Fifth Avenue in twenty-five minutes. Entering the Old Fifth Avenue Hotel from Ninth Street, Sarah and Cassandra walked though the revolving glass doors into the grand foyer and over to the information desk to ask for Ginger. The doorman called up to the suite to announce their arrival. Cassandra was impressed with the lobby, "It's big and pretty. Isn't it, Grandmother?"

"Yes it is, dear." She thought to herself, what a difference from the old gypsy's apartment on Christopher Street. They rode the elevator to the top floor and found Ginger's suite.

Sarah rang the bell, and Ginger, a small, fiftyish woman answered the door. She was beautifully dressed in a tailored grey silk suit. Her short, salt and pepper hair was smartly styled. She smiled and welcomed them inside. "How do you do, Mrs. Collins? So good to see you again. This must be Cassandra! So good to meet you." Ginger hugged Sarah and shook Cassandra's hand. The suite was a penthouse, overlooking Washington Square. It was furnished sleekly, in Art Deco, with gray wall to wall carpet and brass lighting fixtures with frosted, Lalique glass. All the chairs and sofas were covered in an expensive cranberry velvet. To Sarah's experienced eye it was evident that Ginger paid some decorator a small fortune to do it.

Ginger ushered Sarah and Cassandra down a corridor to her office. Her many framed diplomas were on the wall behind a huge glass desk. The office was impeccable and inspired confidence in the woman who worked in it. Her mother would have been so proud to see her daughter in such a wonderful setting. Ginger had learned the psychic arts from her mother, but chose to earn her doctorate in psychology and become a certified therapist. Most of her clients knew nothing of her psychic gifts, and they remained a private matter between herself and her mother's old friends, like Sarah, whom she continued to counsel after her mother's passing.

Ginger was experienced through her psychiatric practice at dealing with children, so she was able immediately to put Cassandra at her ease. As soon as Cassandra entered the office she spied a small museum copy of an Egyptian cat. Ginger saw her eyeing the statue and asked Cassandra, "Do you like my cat, Cassandra?"

Cassandra nodded her head, "Yes, it is just beautiful."

"Well, then, go over and hold it if you like."

"Oh, could I, Grandmother?" she joyfully looked to Sarah. "Of course, dear. Miss Veilo said it was fine."

As Cassandra looked at the statue of the cat, a strange look came over her face. Ginger noticed the change of expression and asked Cassandra if she would tell her what she was seeing or feeling. "I can see you like the cat, Cassandra. Does it seem familiar to you?"

"Why, yes, it does. I don't have anything at home like it, but it seems like I have had it before." A puzzled look came over the child's face. Ginger said, "That is true, Cassandra. A long time, a very long time ago, you had one just like it in Egypt. This one is a copy from one in the Metropolitan Museum, but the one you had was real and was made for you by an Egyptian sculptor." Sarah realized Ginger was tuning in psychically to another lifetime of Cassandra's. It was one she had had centuries before.

"Mrs. Collins, your granddaughter was a temple seer for the Pharaoh in the Fifth Dynasty, the one his people said was "kissed by the gods." That is why she will be so gifted again in this life."

Sarah had known all along there was something special about Cassandra. Cassandra was able to read her mind, and although Sarah wasn't sure whether she believed in reincarnation, it sounded like the only plausible explanation for this child's uncanny perceptions. Ginger handed the child a worn deck of tarot cards wrapped in silk cloth and instructed her to close her eyes and tell what she was seeing. Cassandra took the deck, closed her eyes, and began speaking. "It is kind of dark. I see an old lady by a fire. She has dark brown eyes and gray hair.

There are many people who come from all over to hear what she has to say."

"Very good, Cassandra. May I have the cards back?"

Cassandra handed the cards back to Ginger and the therapist calmly withdrew a cigarette from a silver box on her desk and offered one to Sarah, who graciously declined. "Mrs. Collins, your granddaughter has described my grandmother who owned these cards. She always read them by a fire in the old country." She looked at Cassandra closely, "Do you always see pictures when you close your eyes, Cassandra?'

"Yes, I do." the child answered.

"Your granddaughter is blessed with clairvoyant sight, Mrs. Collins. She will grow up to be an extremely clear channel. Cassandra, would you like to take the cat home as a present?"

"Yes," she said clutching the cat to her, "very much."

"Good." Ginger was pleased. "Now, my dear, if you will go into the other room for a few moments, I would like to talk privately with your grandmother."

Cassandra took the statue with her into the living room while Sarah and Ginger sat and discussed the child in great depth; Ginger was of the opinion that no special schooling was needed at this time. "Mrs. Collins, Cassandra will be normal in every way. The same as any other little girl. However, as a clairvoyant, she will always be a little more sensitive than others. I would encourage her to study music and art, so she can have an outlet for her creativity. Also, ask her to always discuss whatever is on her mind, especially any dreams she might have."

"Is there anything else I can do for her?"

"She seems happy and content. Just continue to love her and I am sure you will be very proud of her someday."

"Thank you, Dr. Veilo." Sarah wrote her out a generous check. "And thank you so much for the cat, I know how much it will mean to Cassandra."

"You're more than welcome, Mrs. Collins. I felt it already belonged to her."

Chapter Four

The years passed by for Cassandra quickly.

She learned to play the piano and spent many happy hours at the keyboard.

Her music teacher encouraged her to become a professional pianist, but Sarah discouraged the notion, "Darling, there's so much more to life than killing oneself over an instrument, now isn't there?"

Cassandra couldn't argue with her grandmother, besides, there would be no winning. In addition to being naturally bright, Cassandra was able to dream about what would be on the tests when she would study. This ability enabled her to become a straight "A" student. Cassandra became a beautiful young girl. The only trick nature played on her, as it did on many other clairvoyants, was a severe case of myopia which became increasingly worse as she grew older; it was only corrected by very thick glasses, which made her appear studious.

Although not a loner, Cassandra always felt she was different from the other students at the Catholic Girls Academy she attended. By the time she was seven, Tom and Ryan were already off to prep school, so she was raised alone by Sarah, who was already in her late seventies. Her grandmother cautioned Cassandra not to tell outsiders of her clairvoyant gifts, so books became her only real friends besides her grandmother. Though

Cassandra gained wisdom, socially she was not as aware as other girls her age were. This didn't prove a handicap until it was time for her to leave home.

Cassandra never dreamed about boys, as many of the other girls in her class did. She fantasized about a heroic prince, god-like in power and beauty. She loved reading romantic novels by the Bronte sisters knowing in her heart she would someday become the heroine of a real-life drama herself. No pimply-faced adolescent boys for her. She was saving herself for a tall, dark-haired gentleman, who would sweep her off into an exciting world of fantasy, where they could love together and explore the world around them. They would be a couple people would look up to and admire, and they would do great things in the world. And so she endured lonely Saturday nights, patiently waiting for the elusive mystery man to appear.

When it was time for Cassandra to go away to college she decided to go to an all women's school. The guidance counselor at Sacred Heart Academy pushed Trinity College in Burlington, Vermont. Cassandra applied, and received early acceptance with characteristic ease. She was certain she would find what she needed there. In her dreams, I she kept hearing, over and over, the word "Vermont," and since she wouldn't have thought of anything but a Catholic girl's school, it fit together perfectly. So, sight unseen, she made her choice and Fate began to play out its hand.

Upon graduation from high school, Sarah had promised Cassandra that she would take her to Europe for the summer. Cassandra had not anticipated the trip eagerly because something inside told her it would not happen. The week before they were to leave Sarah's blood pressure escalated dangerously high and the doctor advised her not to travel. Sarah was livid; how dare a medical person tell her what she should or shouldn't do. As a result of her anger she suffered a massive cerebral hemorrhage.

Cassandra wasn't surprised: she knew psychically her grandmother was living on borrowed time, just long enough to see her into womanhood. When the doctor told her the gravity of the condition, Cassandra was cool. She called the priest for the last rites of the Church, and then called her brothers to let them know the news. After all the years of observing her grandmother, she knew exactly what to do and how to act. She performed every action as if she were on automatic pilot.

Going home from the hospital, Cassandra paused to find a dead bluebird on her doorstep. She was taken aback, realizing the Irish always believed a dead bird was the harbinger of death. Chills went down her spine, as Cassandra realized Sarah's time had come. The same night Cassandra had a vivid dream. In the dream, Sarah was standing on the bow of a great ocean liner. There was a bon voyage party taking place on board the ship, but Sarah didn't seem in a festive mood. She stood alone, with her back to the other guests, staring out into the ocean. Cassandra approached her, to offer her a glass of champagne, but Sarah declined. In a low voice, she told Cassandra, "My dear, I will always be at your side, even though we seem worlds apart. I am always as near to you as your heart." The dream ended abruptly and Cassandra awoke suddenly and looked at the clock. It was 3 a. m. She knew her grandmother had died. She calmly called the hospital and a nurse answered the phone, telling Cassandra the expected news.

The next day, Cassandra made the funeral arrangements and organized details by herself. The twins were in a daze so she felt she must carry on alone. She handled herself throughout the entire proceedings with poise and never gave way under the strain. Sarah once again was right when she said the women were the backbone of the Collins family. Although in some ways Sarah had sheltered Cassandra, she did a fine job of instilling maturity in her which, combined with her natural grace, gave her an air of authority.

Years later, Cassandra would have almost no recollection of her graduation summer, blocking it out as one does a bad dream. She did, however, develop a severe case of conjunctivitis which no medication seemed able to eradicate. It was not until she went to a prominent Park Avenue eye specialist that she found out the cause of her disease. He asked her if any event in her life coincided with the onset of the malady. When she explained her grandmother died at time of the onset of conjunctivitis, the doctor told her the disease was a sublimation of crying. When she finally grieved the loss of her grandmother, her eyes would clear.

Cassandra was stunned, never once throughout the entire ordeal had she ever shed a tear for the woman she so dearly loved, being afraid that if she started crying, she would never be able to stop. On the way home from the specialist's office, she began crying, and didn't stop for hours. When the crying ceased she regained her composure and was fine.

The family lawyer, an old friend of their father's, convinced Cassandra and the twins to sell the Long Island estate and their grandmother's townhouse. The sales would net over two million dollars.

He would put the jewelry, antiques, and art up for auction. When everything was liquidated, Cassandra would be left with an income of about fifty thousand dollars a year for life.

Despite the chaos that had transpired that summer, Cassandra decided upon going to college as she had planned. Deep inside she knew she would somehow develop her psychic gifts later on, just as Ginger Veilo predicted. Of that she was certain, but for now she would see where life would lead her, setting out like a leaf drifting on the river of life, letting it take her wherever it happened to flow.

Chapter Five

The month before Cassandra left home to begin her first semester of college, National Geographic featured a lush pictorial spread on Vermont in its August issue under the title "God's Country." Cassandra considered this coincidence an excellent omen for the beginning of the next phase of her life. The pictures of the rolling green hills and story book villages helped to lighten the heaviness she had carried around since Sarah's death. She was certain that Vermont's natural beauty would have a healing effect on her strained psyche as she pictured the coming autumn in her mind.

Trinity College was one of four schools in Burlington, a magnificent town set on Lake Champlain in the heart of the Green Mountains. Burlington's many hills and varied terrain proved a great contrast to the flatness of Long Island's south shore where Cassandra was raised. Although Cassandra had traveled to many places around the United States, Canada, Europe and Mexico, and had spent a year abroad with Sarah living in Ireland and England, she had never been away from home alone, not even to summer camp. Tom, sensing Cassandra's need for family ties, decided to take a week's vacation from work and drive Cassandra to school in his station wagon. Cassandra had packed two trunks of clothes: dresses, sweaters, slacks, and blouses of every color and fabric, outfits for every occasion. She wanted to be well-dressed for the fall season, by having everything a college girl could possibly need or want. Tom assured her the monthly allowance from her trust-fund would buy whatever her heart desired. Cassandra, obeying the school rules for freshmen girls, left her blue MG Midget in Tom's garage, waiting until Thanksgiving recess to use it. Together they loaded the back of Tom's Cutlass station wagon and headed north to Vermont.

Cassandra thought it would be a good idea to spend some time alone with Tom before Orientation Week began, so they drove to Burlington a week before school officially opened to settle Cassandra in the dormitory.and have time to do some tourists sites together. They drove to Montreal to the World's Fair, Expo 67, and visited the Von Trapp Lodge in Stowe, Vermont, where they captured a glimpse of the real life Maria from *The Sound of Music*. Cassandra enjoyed getting to know Tom as an adult, an equal. They discussed his life and his business, his relationship to his wife Cathy, and his two daughters, Erin and Eileen. She always felt closer to Tom than Ryan because, although they were twins, they were very different in looks and temperament.

Both were redheads like their grandfather, but Tom was corpulent, easygoing, and optimistic, whereas Ryan was slim, driven, and critical. Both were true to the Collins blood in that they were fabulous money-makers. Their firm was one of the five largest government bond and securities concerns on Wall Street, earning them both millions each year. Very impressive by anyone's standard for two men not yet thirty. Two days before Orientation Week began, Cassandra sent Tom home with a hug and a kiss, thinking him for spending the time with her and making her feel at home.

It was school policy that all first year students share a room, and Cassandra was genuinely looking forward to having a roommate, hoping she would become friends with whoever was assigned her. She wanted them to share the experience of freshman year like sisters. Cassandra was determined to make the year a success both academically and personally so she put her best foot forward to begin the year on a positive note, hoping to blend in with the other students and blot out the summer of Sarah's death like a bad dream.

She used the time before the other girls arrived shopping around town to get the things she needed for her room: a rug, wastebasket, desk lamp, and a few posters for the walls. She decided to wait on purchasing drapes and bedspreads until her roommate arrived. The room itself was very pleasant and had a marvelous view of the crystal clear lake from the window. Cassandra was very pleased with the way things were shaping up. She wasn't, however, prepared for her roommate.

Cassandra was seated on the bed, gazing out at the lake, when she heard a key turn in the door. She turned to see a huge suitcase drop and break open.

"Oh shit! The goddamn strap broke. What luck!"

Her roommate had arrived.

Cassandra jumped up from the bed. "Can I help? I'm your roommate, Cassandra Collins," she said, extending her hand.

"Yeah. Thanks. I'm Elaine Martin. Glad to make your acquaintance. Just help me drag some of this garbage in here, O.K.?"

"Sure," Cassandra said, thinking to herself she had never heard a lady use such language before.

"I hope the boys around here are better than the ones I saw on the way from the airport."

"Didn't your parents drive you up?"

"No." Then, sensing Cassandra's surprise, "It's no big deal. I flew in from Hartford by myself. I mean, I'm eighteen, I'm no baby, and I didn't want the folks to aggravate the crap out of me. You know how crabby parents can be, right?"

Cassandra looked a little bewildered, but nodded affirmatively, "Sure."

"Well, it looks like all my belongings are here," Elaine said, surveying her three suitcases, "Looks like the room is okay, too. Well, now that I'm settled, how about a smoke?" She pulled a pack of Marlboros out of her purse. "I need one bad." She offered one to Cassandra, "You smoke?"

"No, I don't."

"Suit yourself. I don't know what I would do without them," she said, taking a drag. "So, tell me about yourself. Did you say it was Cassandra?

"Yes. "

"Does anyone ever call you Sandy?"

"No. I prefer being called Cassandra."

"Okay by me. Just wanted to know. So how are things, Cassandra?"

Cassandra and Elaine spent the next few hours talking, getting to know one another. Cassandra was a lady in every sense of the word; Sarah's strict but loving upbringing had done its job, Elaine could see that clearly. Elaine, on the other hand, was a flower child, and had "been around." By the age of eighteen, she had already had an abortion, run away with her boyfriend to back-pack through Europe for a summer, dated interracially, and smoked dope. Cassandra realized having Elaine as a roommate was going to be a large part of her education. Elaine wanted to be an actress and was only in college to appease her parents to whom she gave conniption fits. Elaine was their only child, and they, being strict Catholics, felt she would be safe at Trinity, with the good sisters curbing her rebellious goings-on. She had no more interest in higher education than in the man in the moon. Because she didn't want to go to work to support herself, she consented to attend Trinity, her last choice for a school. All the colleges she wanted to attend were in Boston, and none would have her. She figured it would look good on a resume that she had attended college, so what the hell. Elaine thought Cassandra simply had to make Trinity her first choice. With her grades, she could have gone anywhere she wanted to go. The two unlikely roommates were paired up for their first semester and both reacted with good humor, each realizing the total incongruity of the match.

Chapter Six

The first few weeks of school flew by for Cassandra. She loved the courses she was taking and enjoyed the intellectual discipline of study. It seemed to act as a tonic for her grief. She barely thought of home or of Sarah except on some evenings before bedtime. She liked the other girls in the dorm and was excited to be developing friendships with them. She wasn't as anxious to date as some of the more experienced girls, because she hadn't seen or met anyone from the other schools that seemed interesting. On Friday nights, some of the girls would hop on the bus and take a short ride to the mixers at St. Michael's College, an all-male school. A few of the girls met some nice boys, but Cassandra didn't click with them. Their conversations about school and sports failed to interest her, but she would go and listen to them talk just to be sociable.

Elaine on the other hand was bored to tears with school, hated her classes and tried skipping or cutting whenever the opportunity presented itself. She dated almost every chance she had and was the most sociable of all the girls in the freshman class. She snagged a few dates with upper classmen at the fraternity houses of the University of Vermont and was studying at their library in the hope of grabbing one of them as a steady boyfriend.

Elaine was in real trouble academically and needed help badly. When she asked

Cassandra what she thought would be on a test, she was amazed at how often the things Cassandra told her to study showed up.

"Gee, Cassandra, it's amazing how often you read the teacher's mind. It's like you were a witch or something."

"Guess I'm just psychic.'

"Doesn't that scare you?" Elaine asked quizzically.

"No. I have always been able to feel things or sense them before they happened."

"Must come in handy."

"Most times it does except when you feel something bad is about to happen and you don't know how to stop it."

"I imagine it would be kind of funny. Have you always had these feelings?"

"Yes, ever since I was a little girl. Sometimes my grandmother would misplace a thing, and I would know where it was."

"Wow, sounds spooky to me. Maybe you should be on *Twilight Zone* or something."

"I'm sure its perfectly natural. I don't know how it would feel to be any other way."

"I guess we all have our own reality."

"Yes, we do. We all want different things out of life."

"I want to be a star and have a glamorous life, and marry a rich man who will take me around the world, and have a fabulous sex life and tons of money so I'll never have to worry about anything. Doesn't that sound great?"

Cassandra shook her head, "Sure, if that's what you want. To use your own words: we all have our own reality."

"What do you want to do with your life?"

"I don't know exactly, but I feel it will involve some type of counseling or teaching. I like to help people."

"So I've noticed. Why don't you become a nun?"

"No. I want to have a special man share my life, a career, and children. I want it all."

"Sounds dreary to me."

"We are all different, Elaine. That's what makes the world go around."

"Well, you go on and become Donna Reed. I'll be Elizabeth Taylor and when we're both fifty we'll get together and compare notes. Deal?" Elaine stuck her hand out.

Cassandra shook it. "You've got a deal." Cassandra got chills down her spine when she held Elaine's hand. She intuitively knew Elaine would never see thirty years old, and it made her freeze. She forced a smile and was relieved to see Elaine hadn't noticed the change come over her.

Elaine figured she would be able to help Cassandra by teaching her the fine art of makeup, since she wouldn't let her help her find a boyfriend. Elaine found it difficult to believe that any normal college freshman girl was still a virgin, with no man on the horizon. Having been on the pill since her abortion, she was determined to have no more "accidents." She had been sleeping with boys since she was fourteen, and used sex as a tool to get what she wanted. Cassandra wanted no part of Elaine's boyfriends-she wasn't desperate for a hamburger or a movie. Besides, she was going to wait for her prince. She did, however, let Elaine instruct her in cosmetics because Elaine was a wizard when it came to the world of beauty. Elaine always sang, "A little powder and a little paint, makes a girl what she ain't." She owned a subscription to every beauty magazine under the sun. Cassandra swore *Cosmopolitan* was Elaine's Bible.

Elaine was well put together, she was

a walking advertisement for the beliefs she espoused. Her breasts were surgically augmented with silicone implants, her four front teeth were perfectly capped, and her nose was fashionably "bobbed." Adding to this her green-tinted contact lenses and frosted blonde hair, she was a regular minx. Cassandra, on the other hand, was a natural beauty, inheriting her grandmother's porcelain Irish complexion and thick auburn hair. Her only flaw were the thick, coke-bottle glasses that hid her beautiful eyes. Elaine had no trouble convincing Cassandra to get rid of the glasses and be fitted for violet contact lenses. When she was finally used to wearing the new lenses Elaine taught her how to use a mascara wand. Now men couldn't help but stare at Cassandra. She possessed an ethereal beauty that became her passport into the world of romance.

Cassandra dreamed of her prince, a tall, dark young man with incredibly sensitive eyes and a magnificently sculpted body. In the dream, she was walking through flowering fields, holding his hand, feeling pregnant and blissfully happy. When she awoke, she knew she would soon meet this stranger, who would share her life to come. She told no one of the dream, fearing they would discount it as illusion. But in her heart she knew he was out there, waiting to discover her, to find her.

During the first few weeks of school, Cassandra never seemed to want to date, and it wasn't as if the boys didn't try. She just wasn't interested in any of them. She lived increasingly in her own little world of books, classes, and the library, and it simply drove Elaine mad. One afternoon, Elaine dragged Cassandra away from the books to join her over at the University for a basketball practice. Although Cassandra had no interest in sports whatsoever something inside told her to accompany Elaine.

When they got to the gym, Elaine seemed to know all the players and their histories, on and off the court. She had dated one of the players and had gone to some of their parties. Cassandra listened politely, but her mind was thousands of miles away. Until she glimpsed him.

"Who is number 22, Elaine?" Cassandra asked breathlessly.

"Peter Brown. Cute, huh?"

"Yes, he's adorable. I want to meet him."

"Dream on, sister. He's the number one scorer on and off the court, if you get my drift, and besides he's practically engaged to Jane Greenwald. "

"I don't care. I want you to introduce me after practice."

"Okay by me, but it's your funeral."

Cassandra ignored the remark and scrutinized Peter Brown closely. She must meet him. Finally, Elaine could be of help to her.

Later they went downstairs to wait while the players showered. "I hope you know what you're doing, Cassandra."

"What do you mean?"

"Well, Arthur Stone has been wanting to date you for over two weeks, and he's on the team, too."

"Elaine, I couldn't care less about Arthur Stone. Are you going to introduce me to Peter, or am I going to have to introduce myself?"

"I told you I'd do it, but I don't understand the big rush."

"Don't worry about it. Just introduce us, please."

"Okay."

As Peter left the locker room, Cassandra nudged Elaine, "Here he comes. Get up and introduce us."

Elaine reluctantly got up and put on

her best and phoniest smile. "Why, Peter Brown," she said, extending her hand, "We met last week at the toga party. Elaine Martin."

"How are you Elaine? And how is Stuart Edleman?"

"Oh, I haven't seen him this week. I've been busy studying." Cassandra nudged Elaine. "Oh. And this is my roommate, Cassandra."

"Glad to make your acquaintance." Peter was taken aback. This girl, unlike her roommate Elaine, was no groupie. His heart pounded as he made small talk with them. "Nice to see you, Elaine. I'll tell Stuart I ran into you."

"Don't bother, really, I prefer being a free woman."

Peter thought to himself, very free, if you believe campus talk.

"Cassandra, I have to get back to the dorm. I'm expecting a very important phone call," said Elaine.

Cassandra was staring at Peter. "Oh, you go on then, Elaine. I'm going over to the pizza place to have a Coke."

"See you later," Elaine waved, sauntering away.

"Mind if I join you?" Peter asked.

"No, I'd love it if you would," Cassandra said, flashing her biggest smile, showing off her dimples to perfection.

Elaine was amazed. She had always assumed Cassandra was shy.

Cassandra wasn't shy. When she wanted something she went after it, after all, she wasn't Sarah's granddaughter for nothing.

Peter walked Cassandra over to the Big Ben Pizza Parlor and ordered two Cokes. Cassandra smiled, "When I saw you, I just had to meet you," she said, turning a bright shade of crimson.

"Don't explain yourself. I'm glad you did."

"Elaine told me who you were, and I said to myself, nothing ventured, nothing gained."

"And here we are." He smiled, gazing into her deep, violet-blue eyes. Cassandra had never in her life seen or met such a handsome man. He was gorgeous in every sense of the word. His eyes were a clear hazel framed by thick black lashes, and his skin, unlike her fair complexion, was naturally dark and deeply tanned. His face showed great sensitivity; Cassandra felt in her heart that he was good to the core. She felt blessed to be with him.

"So, tell me about yourself," Peter asked.

"Like what? I don't know what to tell."

"Well, I know your first name is Cassandra, and that you look like a dream sent from heaven, but otherwise I know nothing about you. "

Cassandra giggled. He was naturally curious about her, as she was about him. She wasn't nervous, however; his quiet strength immediately put her at ease. "My full name is Cassandra Collins. I am eighteen years old, and a freshman at Trinity College majoring in liberal arts." Peter was hanging on every word she said. "I am from Long Island." She smiled and sipped her Coke, playing with the straw.

Peter thought to himself, if she's from Trinity College, she isn't Jewish, but that didn't bother him. He had never encountered such a beautiful girl before, Jewish or not. He felt his gold Star of David hanging around his neck and realized that although his family would not like him dating a non-Jew, he was already smitten with her, and he didn't care if she was an Arab; she was lovely and he was interested.

"Well, that was a short bio. What would you like to know about me, in twenty-five words or less?"

Cassandra smiled, "Everything."

"Well in that case, I suggest we have dinner tomorrow night. I've got an important bio lab in half an hour that I can't miss. How does that strike you?"

"Great . "

"What is your number?"

Cassandra gave him her number.

"I've got to run." He put on his coat and placed his hand on Cassandra's, "See you tomorrow about eight."

She smiled and turned as he went out the door. She was unable to move so she just sat there and watched him through the window as he crossed the hill and disappeared from sight.

Chapter Seven

The University of Vermont was an interesting society in the late Sixties. There were farm children studying agricultural science, learning scientific farming, so they could supply their New England neighbors with better vegetables and more milk. Then there were the children of the professional people of Vermont, using the university as a launching pad for careers in law, education, and medicine. Finally, there were the wealthy, out-of-state students who used the university as an educational St. Moritz, to obtain degrees while becoming great skiers.

Peter Brown was from a family whose wealth was from manufactured New England leather goods. Although his ancestors didn't arrive on the Mayflower, they managed to escape from a Polish ghetto and secure passage to the United States in the eighteen nineties, settling in Boston. Peter's paternal grandfather, Isadore Kominsky, was a shoemaker, who successfully plied his trade with old world excellence and dedicated craftsmanship. His innate business sense and sparkling blue eyes gave him a thriving shoe repair business. With the money he saved, he saw that his son, Samuel, took advantage of all New England's educational opportunities.

Upon graduating from Harvard, Samuel Kominsky changed his name to the good New England name of Sam Brown, and with his father's savings began a shoe and leather goods manufacturing company. Within ten years he became a very wealthy man. Through dealings in the Jewish community of greater Boston, he happened to meet and fall in love with Helene Schaff, daughter of one of his father's fellow Polish immigrants. Helene was blessed with beauty and grace, and, after an engagement period of a year, they married to the combined joy of their families.

Nine months after the wedding, Helene gave birth to their first child, a healthy eight-pound baby boy, Peter, and their lives were blessed by the child's presence. Until his two sisters were born, Helene never understood why women complained about infants. Peter was a model child, having a perfect disposition, he never had cholic, slept at regular intervals, and was easy to potty train. He never gave her a minute's trouble.

Growing up is never easy for anyone, but Peter seemed to make the transition from adored child, strong in a family of love, trust, and education, to responsible adult, as easily as anyone could. He was a unique man, one who possessed the gifts of charm, good looks, intelligence, and charisma, and yet he remained unspoiled and unaffected. The fact of the matter was he was also basically naive. He was a friend to all who befriended him, and was so busy with his studies and athletic pursuits that he never had time to think there might be people who didn't like him.

The world was open to Peter, and whatever he chose to do. He was class valedictorian and voted "Most Likely to Succeed" by his prep school graduating class. There wasn't a doubt in anyone's mind that he would attain greatness. Peter decided early to become a psychiatrist. He was determined nothing would stand in his way.

His family was delighted when he decided to enroll at the University of Vermont. The school was within driving distance of home, so they would see him often. During his first three years of school he came home regularly. Many girls had fallen in love with Peter over the years, but his mother jokingly referred to them as Cinderella's sisters. Peter dated around and, by most people's standards, had an enviable sex life. But he never had anyone make an impact on his psyche until he met Cassandra. He knew upon meeting her he was in the presence of royalty, a Princess in every way equal to himself-except in the matter of religion. From the first time he saw her, she was constantly on his mind, smiling, radiant, beautiful. He knew he had met his match, and it made him feel good, though vaguely uneasy. The man who always had all the answers was now in a space where there was someone else to consider, someone he didn't even know.

Cassandra was excited about her first date with Peter, which was her first actual date with anyone. Oh, she had been on group outings in school and to church related events, but she had never been asked out by herself. She blushed to remember she had to beg her brothers to have one of their friends escort her to the high school senior prom. Now things would be different. Peter would change all that.

Cassandra spent over an hour getting ready, making certain she looked her best. She manicured her nails, gave herself an egg white facial, and deep-conditioned her hair, setting it with hot rollers in a beautiful swept-back style. She was exhilarated like she had been

been as a child expecting the arrival of Santa Claus and his goodies. She savored the lovely feelings she was experiencing and was literally singing with joy. All the doubts of her existence faded into the background as she left the joyous mood overtake her. She wore a blue silk blouse, with a simple strand of Cartier pearls and a pair of gray cashmere slacks.

Elaine was at once both amused and annoyed by Cassandra's mood. She said, in a patronizing tone, "You act as if you never had a date before."

Cassandra thought to herself, if she only knew the truth. "Oh, darling, Prince Charming is coming to take me out and Cinderella will shine tonight," she said, smiling, "Wish me luck."

"What kind?" Elaine said in her smart ass tone.

Cassandra didn't respond to the sarcastic comment; she realized Elaine was jealous of her date with Peter, but she refused to let it upset her.

Elaine was back to reading one of her beauty magazines, and, without looking up, said, "See you later," all the while wishing it were she and not

Cassandra who was dating the humpy Mr. Peter Brown.

"Bye." Cassandra flew out of the room and waltzed down the hall as if she were floating on air. She crossed her fingers for luck and took one last look in the large mirror at the top of the staircase before taking a deep breath and descending the staircase to meet her prince.

Peter was anxiously awaiting Cassandra downstairs in the lounge with the other young men who were waiting to pick up their dates for the evening. He felt slightly ridiculous over his nervousness, after all, he had been through this scene before, and he wasn't called "Mr. Cool" for nothing. Nevertheless, his palms were sweating, and his heart was racing. Although the feeling was uncomfortable, it was also exciting and enticing, previewing the magic the evening ahead held in store. He had never before experienced the feelings Cassandra's presence had evoked within him. She was different from all the girls he had known previously. As the adrenaline rushed through his veins, he looked up to see Cassandra descending the staircase, and as he rose to greet her, he realized the feeling inside might be what those romantic fools called love. "Cassandra," he said, taking her arm, "You look beautiful."

"Thank you, Peter. You don't look too bad yourself," she said jokingly. Peter looked simply great in his light brown suede jacket and casual v-neck cashmere sweater and khaki pants. Cassandra said, "Let me sign out." She went over to the big ledger at the nun's desk by the switchboard and signed her name and the time. Under the ledger heading of activity, she wrote, "The Prince's Ball, escorted by Peter Brown." She smiled to herself as she left the desk. "Where are we off to?"

"I thought maybe a movie and grab a bite to eat afterwards. How does that sound to you?"

"Fine, but I have to be in around midnight. If we go to a movie, we won't have much time to talk and get to know each other. "

"You're right. Let's just go down to Henry's Diner. We'll do the movie this weekend. "

Cassandra liked his style: he had already arranged for another date without having to ask. Although Peter was polished, she felt a deep sensitivity underneath his veneer.

Burlington was a college town, swarming with men and women in their late teens and early twenties; dating, falling in love, and planning futures together. Cassandra and Peter were no different from any of the other young couples. Romance was in the air and they were as intoxicated with it and each other as the rest of the young lovers who populated the magical city on Lake Champlain.

Peter's bright red Mustang convertible was parked outside the dormitory. He opened the door for Cassandra and they headed down to the old tree-lined street the separated Trinity College from the University. Peter was proud of his car. It was a graduation present from his parents and, although it was getting cooler in the evenings, he still kept the top down. Cassandra tied a silk scarf around her long, auburn tresses and Peter playfully untied it as they sped into town.

"I want to see your hair blowing in the breeze."

"Your wish is my command," Cassandra joked.

"That could be dangerous."

"I believe in living dangerously . . . sometimes. Besides, I trust you, Peter," Cassandra said, testing the waters.

"You are direct, Cassandra, and I like the quality very much."

"I want us to get to know each other."

"I feel as if I do know you, Peter. From somewhere inside it's just getting acquainted we need to do. Does that make sense?"

"Yes, in some crazy way it does. I know what you mean."

As they pulled up in front of the little restaurant, Cassandra noticed the movie playing across the street at the State Theatre was Zefferilli's *Romeo and Juliet*. She hoped they would not be starcrossed like Shakespeare's tragic pair.

Peter came around to her side of the car and opened the door.

"Chivalry is not dead," Cassandra remarked, smiling.

"No, only sleeping, waiting to be reborn for a princess."

Cassandra loved being with a man who indulged her wish for a fairy tale relationship without having to be told. Yes, it seemed like Mr. Peter Brown was her prince.

Peter had lasagna and salad, reflecting a passion for Italian food. Cassandra ordered broiled sea bass with rice. They shared a carafe of white wine over the main course.

The evening flew by as Peter did most of the talking, telling Cassandra of his family, his life in Boston, and his plans for the future as a psychiatrist at a teaching hospital. Cassandra hung on every word as if it were coming from an oracle instead of a twenty-one year old student. As she gazed intently into his eyes, Peter realized his search for the perfect woman was over. It was a classic case of love at first sight for them both, and it had every sign of deepening and ripening into something good and everlasting. Peter hadn't even been to bed with her, yet he was willing to share his life with this stranger whom he felt he had always know. It was too much for his rational mind to comprehend.

After talking for over three hours, Cassandra finally noticed the time. She must get back in time for the midnight curfew, otherwise she would have hell to pay with Sister Chastity Maureen. Peter paid the check and they drove the short distance back to her dorm.

Peter parked his car on the street and

turned to Cassandra. "This has been a perfect evening. I want to see more of you. How about Saturday night?"

"You're on."

Peter held her in his arms and gave her a good night kiss that was beautiful, sincere, and at the same time sensual. Cassandra savored his lips and was transfigured by her feelings. If she had any doubts they all vanished with his kiss. She pulled herself away, just in time for the curfew. Peter got out of the car, and escorted her to the door. As she entered the doorway, she blew him a kiss. The delightful, little girl action warmed his heart. He had "it" bad, and "it" felt good.

Peter drove back to the University of Vermont campus and parked his car In the large lot behind the dorm where he had spent the last three years of his college life. As he walked up to his room, he was hoping his roommate, Ed, would still be up studying so they could talk.

Their dorm was typical for the university: two single beds, two beat-up desks, two chairs and two dressers. Both Peter and Ed were jocks, so the only decorations in the room were a University of Vermont banner, a Boston Red Sox pennant, a

Budweiser beer sign, and the latest Playmate of the Month hung on the back of the door. It was in this room they lived their lives apart from the rest of the university. It was here they brought their dates, did their studying, discussed their futures, and slept. It was the only place to be alone when you needed some peace.

Ed was out at the library studying for an exam so Peter would have to wait until tomorrow to tell him about his date with Cassandra. Ed and Peter did a lot of talking. They came together freshman year assigned to the same room and hit if off immediately. They soon became best buddies even though they were entirely different. Ed Hansen came from Ludlow, a small town in western Massachusetts, complete with a town square, a church, school, post office and fire department. He was raised in the traditional New England way, with its values firmly embedded in his consciousness: work hard, study at a good school, go to church on Sundays, play by the rules, marry a good woman, then by the sweat of your brown rise to a position of honor in your community. Then you will enjoy the fruits of your labor with your family by your side.

Ed never cared to question the beliefs that were his foundation. He was a product of his family, culture, and society. While other students were letting their hair grow long, smoking dope, protesting the Vietnam war and generally flipping out, Ed studied hard, maintained a B+ average, and was unmoved by the world outside his immediate concerns.

Peter, on the other hand, being the child of a cosmopolitan Boston family, was exposed to a very liberal Jewish education and was politically aware of every nuance in the news. He was raised to believe that hard work was the foundation of success, but everyday savvy or know-how was the trick to staying on top. After all, the Jews had survived by their wits in this hostile world and Peter was never one to forget it. Those who ignored the handwriting on the wall perished in the Holocaust. Peter and his family were survivors who would never let ill fate befall them. Peter had no doubt he would become a famous psychiatrist, wealthy, well-traveled, socially prominent, with a beautiful wife and brilliant children.

He wanted the best that life had to offer, and he was hell-bent on acquiring it.

He believed it was his right as one of God's chosen people, and this winning attitude affected everything he did. When he met Cassandra, he sized up the situation and, after seeing what he wanted, went after it. He did, however, like to take all points of view into consideration, therefore he valued Ed's opinions. Although Ed was provincial in his judgments, he spoke sincerely and was a man to be trusted.

The next day Peter discussed his feelings about Cassandra with Ed. Ed was supportive of the relationship but cautioned him to move slowly. Peter listened carefully to the advice, but trying to slow down was an impossibility. He listened but ignored the warning.

The weeks passed by quickly, and the relationship between Peter and Cassandra grew more intense. Peter dropped his other girlfriends, including Jane Greenwald, lovely as she was. None could evoke the feelings he had when he was with Cassandra. Everyone noticed the change in Peter, especially Ed. One afternoon, after basketball practice, Ed came into the room seeing Peter lying on his bed, staring off into space.

"Man, you are really hooked. The next thing , you'll be talking about marriage."

Peter smiled to himself. "Yeah, maybe I will."

"I never thought the king of rock and roll would want to settle down. Miracles never cease." Ed mockingly pronounced.

Peter answered, "Live and learn, my friend, we must live and learn."

"Sounds more like romance than philosophy to me."

"Romance 101, and I intend to get an 'A,' with Cassandra grading all my papers."

"And I bet you'll just love doing the homework and research reports."

"Right on," Peter laughed.

Chapter Eight

It was easy for Cassandra to adapt to her life with Peter. She attended classes all morning and she spent most afternoons in the library studying and reading up on her assignments. She made up her mind on majoring in Psychology because, as a professional psychic, it would be useful in her future career.

Elaine seemed far more distant now since Peter was the center of her life. Elaine had many dates but no one seemed to last past the first or second date. Elaine hated the small time attitude of college "boys"; she planned to quit school and go to work for the airlines if she wasn't expelled first. She slept late, missed classes, and because the teachers were nuns she was unable to ply her superficial charm, which they easily saw through.

Midterms were scheduled before Thanksgiving recess, and some of the girls in the dorm were worried. Elaine was really nonplussed about the whole thing, she figured she'd fail almost everything anyhow and get booted out, but the cynic in her forced her to ask Cassandra what she thought might be on the philosophy exam.

"Tell me what you think Sister Goofball is going to ask on the phil test, Cassandra. I have a bet with some of the girls it will be a multiple guess extravaganza."

"If I were you, I'd change my bet. I feel it will be an essay test on Hindu philosophy, focusing on karma and reincarnation."

"Really?"

"Yes, Sister Gwendolyn Claire has a special interest in India. I could feel it when she was lecturing."

"You don't think she really believes

we come back as animals, now do you?"

"If you didn't cut all the morning lectures you'd know that is not reincarnation but transmigration. No educated Indians believe we come back as animals, but, like Teilhard de Chardin, they believe man is on an evolutionary spiral upward toward the Creator, and we have to go through many successive lifetimes before we become perfect."

"Sounds like Charles Darwin to me. Look out Tarzan."

"In a way it is. Just call it spiritual evolution and you have the whole concept."

"What do you think karma is, then?"

"Karma is the universal law of balance. Whatever one does comes back to him, for good or evil."

"Got it. What goes around, comes around."

"Yes, it really is like that," Cassandra agreed.

"You sound like you believe this stuff."

"Makes more sense to me than the other things I was taught about hell with devils torturing everybody with pitchforks."

"Yeah, well I personally think the

whole thing is a crock, I mean, when you're dead, you're dead."

"To each his own, as my grandmother said."

"The way you always quote your grandmother, she must have been some kind of philosopher."

"I guess in her own way she was," Cassandra said, smiling. "I must get back to studying."

"Well, I'm going out with a few of the other girls for some pizza, and let you geniuses alone. By the way, where's Peter?"

"Oh, he's studying for his inorganic chemistry exam so he figured he didn't need any extra distractions until exams were over."

"Well, it's the first time you've studied here in three weeks, just thought I'd check it out."

"Don't worry about me, everything is great."

"Okay. So long."

"See you later." As Elaine left the room, Cassandra thought to herself how right she was: everything was fine now with Peter in her life.

Cassandra didn't want Peter to think of her as "weird" or crazy, but she did have the need to share her innermost feelings with him, and she trusted him, more than she believed possible. When they discussed their future she was thrilled, because she believed they were meant for happiness together. When she told Peter of her psychic feelings, he was fascinated. His interest in psychology complemented her blooming awareness of another dimension to life and she was relieved when he said he had read of psychics and their gifts in a course he studied on parapsychology. Cassandra didn't feel that she needed to keep secrets from Peter, knowing he would be on her side.

Autumn was magical in every way for Cassandra; her only dread was going home for Thanksgiving because it meant being away from Peter. She had promised Ryan and his wife, Betty, that she would spend the holiday with them. It was understood Peter would go home to Boston to spend the holidays with his family. She loved Peter more and more every day, and although she hadn't "gone all the way" with him, she felt inside that it would be right. When he asked her to spend a weekend away in a motel in Burlington, she said yes, and her heart was filled with joy.

Chapter Nine

Cassandra's heart was pounding so loud in her breast that she was convinced Peter would hear it. Sensing her anxiety, he held her hand. The Holiday Inn in Burlington was not exactly the castle Snow White was swept off to.

Peter had been with dozens of girls before, but none as special as Cassandra. Checking into the motel, Cassandra's face turned a bright crimson. Peter signed the register "Mr. and Mrs. Peter Brown." Cassandra stared at the names in ink; she wished in her heart it were so. The middle-aged male clerk seemed nonplussed, he was just happy the whole transaction was cash.

Peter was inwardly joyful, but he sensed something was not right with Cassandra. "What's wrong, hon?" He asked with a quizzical look on his face.

"Nothing really, Peter. I just always thought I would only be doing this after I was married," she replied shyly.

"Cassandra, tell me honestly, is this your first time?"

Embarrassed by the directness of the question but at the same time relieved, Cassandra confessed, "Yes."

"Well, this calls for a celebration," Peter said with a devilish grin on his face, "We'll go to the room and check our suitcases, then go out to the Rathskeller for a bite to eat."

"Peter, you're so sweet. I don't know what to say."

Squeezing her hand, he picked it up and kissed it. "Don't say anything."

Although it was only November, it was snowing outside. At this moment the world seemed clean and quiet. Cassandra believed herself to be the luckiest girl on the face of the earth. Peter opened the door of his red Mustang and let her in, brushing her cheek with a kiss. They drove down the snowy road three miles to the Rathskeller Restaurant. It was downstairs in an aged building near the quaint New England square in the center of town. Because of the weather it wasn't crowded, and the maitre d' sat them in the corner away from other people, where they could just stare at the fire and dream. The candlelight atmosphere completed the mood. Although Cassandra wasn't ln the slightest big hungry, she ordered chicken Divan. Peter's appetite was always ravenous, so he ordered a filet mignon with a magnum of Dom Perignon. When Cassandra raised her eyebrow, he just smiled, "Don't worry I've got my father's American Express card."

Peter poured her glass of champagne and then filled his own.

"To Cassandra, May our lives be kissed by the gods. " As he clinked the glasses a chill went down her spine. "Is everything all right? You look like you've seen a ghost."

"Oh, Peter, everything is more than fine," tears were coming to her eyes, "Everything is wonderful."

All though the dinner Cassandra mused to herself of the toast, as prophecy, a good omen, she thought. It seemed a beautiful dream and she never wanted to wake up.

After dinner, they returned, arm in arm, to the motel room. Peter went in to shower and use the bathroom first. When he came out, totally nude, Cassandra felt a lump in her throat.

Although she had seen him on the basketball court, she never realized how beautiful he would look naked. A Greek god could never have been more perfect, more beautiful than this powerful man who stood before her in all his natural glory. His muscled body looked like the Michelangelo David she had seen on her first trip to Florence, but the golden tan of his skin was even more spectacular than the marble statue; the glow in his eye was almost more than she could bear.

When she was in the bathroom she heard a knock on the door. Peter answered, "Don't worry, I'll get it." She stood in the shower and closed her eyes, seeing a spray of roses in her mind's eye. Peter had ordered a dozen red roses for her. She stepped out of the shower and drenched herself in Chanel No. 5, put on her silk negligee, and turned the light out behind her as she entered the room.

"Who was that?" Cassandra asked coyly.

"The florist," he said, handing her one of the perfect, long stemmed roses. Tears filled Cassandra's eyes, and they kissed.

Peter carried her to the king-sized bed and lay her down. He then undid the top button of her nightgown as he nuzzled her ear and neck. Cassandra was in a whirl. She felt warm and fuzzy. A moistness crept between her legs and she squeezed her eyes closed. Peter whispered in her ear to relax and continued undressing her. He pulled the covers off the bed and slid beside her beneath the sheets. He then began to cover her from head to toe with little kisses. Cassandra held him tight as he fondled her beautifully formed breasts. He put each nipple between his lips and licked and sucked them gently.

Cassandra felt transported on waves of love and her body began to glow. He then dropped down to her belly and tickled her with his tongue, teasing her in a playful manner, then he went back to her neck and mouth. He kissed her with such love and passion that she at last understood the passion of Lady Chatterly, Romeo and Juliet, and every romantic novel she ever read. Fairytales do come true, she thought.

He was an expert in the art of love, having had plenty of experience, but he had never had anyone as lovely or exciting as the partner that now lay open and vulnerable in his arms. He wanted to love her, protect her, and at the same time devour her; the man who always prided himself on total control on and off the basketball court was now not himself, but a loving animal possessed by some uncontrollable passion that he didn't understand, but loved. He dropped down to her pubic area and started gently nibbling her. He put his tongue inside her and licked and sucked as if he were a man dying of thirst. Cassandra began to writhe and moan.

Peter then climbed back onto her breast and thrust his cock, which was near to exploding, inside her. He felt her jerk as he tore the hymen, and the pleasure/pain was almost too exquisite for Cassandra to bear. His rhythmic thrusting brought her to orgasm almost immediately and she astrally projected out of her body. The two became as one as his semen spurted into her body and mingled with her virgin blood.

Cassandra felt an emotion she never knew existed, Peter had not only deflowered her, but captured her soul and all she wanted to do was retain the magic of that moment forever.

Chapter Ten

The next morning Cassandra awoke in Peter's arms, and realized her life would never be the same. She loved him totally, body, heart, and soul, and knew her future was intertwined with his. She watched him sleep and didn't dare move for fear of waking him; she was totally at peace staring at his handsome face, now looking like a slumbering cherub in the morning's golden light.

When Peter finally awoke, he kissed her good morning and they faced the day together. Peter planned on driving to Stowe for the weekend and staying at a lodge there until Sunday night. The snow had stopped and driving was safe, so they decided to go after a leisurely breakfast in bed. Thank God for room service.

The roses from the night before were beginning to unfold, and their perfume filled the room. After breakfast, they got ready for the afternoon drive, and before they left the room, Cassandra gathered the roses along with her overnight case, and waited for Peter to get the car.

The weekend passed by quickly. Each one realized how right they were for each other and how blessed they were to be sharing the time together. Even though neither of them verbalized it, they knew they were in love. Sunday evening came much too soon as they drove back to Burlington in time for classes the next morning. They would only be able to see each other for a few hours because of heavy schedules, and on Wednesday both had to leave for home for Thanksgiving. The knowledge of the separation only seemed to make their time together seem more precious.

Arriving back at the dorm Peter ran into Ed just about to leave to go have a few beers with some of the other guys in the dorm.

"Hey, man, how was your weekend?

"Great, we had a wonderful time."

"Why don't you drop your gear and come on over to the Den with Jimmy and Bob for a few brews and we can talk about it."

"I'd really like to, but I can't."

Ed was aware that Peter was really infatuated over Cassandra. "Gee, you haven't been out with the guys in over three weeks. Are you pussy whipped or something?"

"What do you mean?"

"You know. You're the one who always says you have time for what's really important, right?"

"Yeah, well, Ed, you've known me for three years, probably as well as anyone does. I guess my feelings for Cassandra are more important than going out with the guys for a few beers. This is too important for me to mess it up, and besides, I think I will marry Cassandra."

"And what does she say about your decision?"

"I haven't asked her yet."

"Then what makes you so sure she'll say yes?"

"Trust me, I know."

"Okay. I'll tell the guys, our first friend bites the dust."

"Yes, tell them. Go on."

"So long, lover boy." Ed laughed as he left the room. Peter realized that Ed was right, he was a goner and he didn't care, it felt so good, so right, with Cassandra beside him he could conquer the world. His parents he wasn't so sure of, but the world, of course. After all, didn't his mother always say that behind every great man was a great woman? Well, he believed he had met his, and he didn't think he would meet any resistance from Cassandra. No, he didn't think he would have any at all.

Thanksgiving proved to be a strange time for both Cassandra and Peter. Both were expected to put in appearances at their families for the holiday. Cassandra was spending it on Long Island with her brother Ryan and his proper socialite wife, Betty. Cassandra didn't relish the idea at all. She would much prefer to be spending it with Peter and his family in Boston or with her brother Tom and his wife Cathy, but both seemed to be impossibilities. Peter hadn't told his family he was dating her, and he explained he needed time to tell them he was dating a Catholic girl.

Tom and Cathy were spending the weekend with her family in New Jersey and she wasn't invited. Ryan had a huge home in Great Neck and he had a beautiful guest room where she was always welcome. She knew they loved her but they had nothing in common and she felt vaguely uncomfortable there. Betty was from a wealthy Westchester family and had been raised to be a princess from birth. Cassandra was frankly bored by Betty and her friends, and all Ryan seemed to know about were Wall Street and sports, two things she was totally disinterested in. They didn't read books or go to the movies, or, she sometimes smugly believed, even think an original thought.

A most upsetting incident happened one night after her grandmother had died. She was spending the night at their home and overheard them discussing her. Because of Cassandra's psychic "intuitions," Betty thought her to be weird, and believed she needed a psychiatrist's care. The hurt worsened when Ryan agreed. Cassandra felt betrayed. They only tolerated her as some kind of rare creature to be kind to, to be pitied. It made her Irish blood boil to think anyone would pity her. She wanted to tell them all about her love for Peter, but she realized they would never understand nor approve her dating a Jew.

In contrast, Peter had a loving family. Still he didn't know how to break the news of being in love with Cassandra and wanting to marry her. It was understood he would finish med school before venturing into the state of holy matrimony—with a good Jewish girl from the Boston area. His family didn't care how many coeds he screwed away from home in Vermont, his father always said, "A man can zip his fly and become a gentleman in the morning." Now Peter didn't intend losing the girl of his dreams because of religious difference. Being Catholic, they might never accept her. They were fine for friends, but a shiksa daughter-in-law? Never. His grandfather would do cartwheels in his grave.

•

The weather forecast for the Wednesday before Thanksgiving was bad, so Peter decided to fly home to Boston instead of taking the five-hour drive in treacherous weather. He would drive Cassandra to the airport, and spend a few more hours with her before they parted for the weekend. When he heard the weather conditions, he immediately phoned her. Trinity College didn't allow the girls to have private phones in their rooms. There were only two public phones on each floor. When he called, both phones were busy. He decided to throw on some clothes and go over to the dorm to catch her before she left.

Just as Peter was pulling up in his car he saw several girls leaving the dorm boarding the mini van going to the airport; Cassandra was one of the group. He circled around the drive and hopped out of the car, and, right before Cassandra entered the bus, she spotted him.

"Peter." She dropped her bag and ran over to him. They embraced .

"Good luck, Cass, I'll be seeing you off at the plane."

"That's great, but won't you be late?"

"No, I've decided to fly home, and leave the car in Burlington."

"What time is your flight?"

"I'm flying standby, so we can spend more time together. Let's go have some hot chocolate."

"Sounds good to me."

Cassandra got into Peter's car and they left the other girls at the van. As they were leaving, Elaine Martin was coming out of the dorm just in time to see Peter and Cassandra kiss then speed off down the road. She wasn't happy for Cassandra. In her jealous heart, she wished she had a boyfriend to take her to the airport instead of the school's lousy mini van.

It started to snow lightly as Peter and Cassandra made their way into town. It was the light, beautiful flurry native Vermonters call sugar snow. Peter and Cassandra were smiling and laughing until Cassandra suddenly stopped laughing and said, "Peter, slow down and get into the right lane." He did exactly as she said without even thinking. Seconds later, the car in front of them had a blowout and screeched over into the inside lane skidding into where they would have been. A cold sweat broke out on Peter's forehead.

"How did you know that?"

"Just saw it before it happened." Cassandra was visibly shaken. "Sometimes, it's good to be psychic."

"I'll say."Peter composed himself and they pulled off the road into a little diner. As Peter opened the door a snowflake landed on Cassandra's eyelashes. Peter stooped and kissed it off, and whispered in her ear, "I love you."

Cassandra looked him straight in the eye, "Peter Brown, I love you, too."

Somewhere inside, Peter felt Cassandra was protected by some powerful unseen force and it both fascinated and disturbed him. He brushed the thought aside as he opened the door to the diner.

They had a small brunch of French toast with hot chocolate, Cassandra's favorite drink. Coffee made her crazy with the caffeine, but she loved the feelings she had with hot chocolate. She took after her grandmother, who had been addicted to Godiva chocolates and Toucher's Chocolate Champagne Truffles. It had been Cassandra's only weakness before she met Peter.

After finishing their meal, Peter reluctantly noticed the time and drove Cassandra to her flight. It was on schedule, so they said their good-byes. He took out some texts and boned up on inorganic chemistry. Although smitten with Cassandra, he intended to stay a straight-A student. He wasn't forgetting his commitment to his future in psychiatric medicine. As he opened up the book he realized once again how good Cassandra was for him. Never once in the eight weeks they dated had she ever discouraged him from studying; quite the contrary, she always made certain that she never took him away from his books. Her responsibility was unlike any other girl he had dated. He was sure she would make the perfect wife. All that was left was to convince his family of her worth. Oh well, he thought, in time they would accept her; he couldn't worry about it now.

Chapter Eleven

Ryan waited at LaGuardia Airport for Cassandra. He wanted to make an effort for her to feel at home. On this first visit from school Cassandra was exhausted. The trip home, plus the drain of the near miss on the interstate with Peter, had tired her. After greeting Betty and the children, she had a light dinner and excused herself to go to bed early.

Cassandra was dreaming of a beautiful diamond engagement ring; it was sparkling in the sun, when suddenly an ominous black cloud swept it away and broke it into a million pieces. She was so shaken by the dream she woke in a cold sweat, hoping it was merely a dream brought on by fatigue. Surely nothing would destroy her happiness now. She rolled over and went back into a fitful sleep, dismissing the first dream as an irrational nightmare. She knew she wouldn't sleep soundly until she saw Peter once again. Then she dreamed of Ryan's children suffocating in the back seat of his car. She awoke to the lingering smell of her grandmother's lavender perfume. She reminded herself to warn him of the premonition in the morning.

Because Peter didn't book a reservation, he had to fly standby to Boston which could mean, with the holiday crunch, he would be lucky to get the six-thirty flight or the last one at ten forty-five. He finally made the last flight, and called before boarding to let his family know he'd be in around midnight. His youngest sister, Susan, wanted to go out to Logan Airport to get a chance to talk with him before all the relatives descended upon him like vultures on Thanksgiving Day. She needed the opportunity to spend time with him before he was worn out talking to friends and relatives. She left their family's beautiful, two-storied brick Georgian home in Lynne, and made the forth-five minute drive to Logan in her father's black Mercedes sedan. Susan thought how lucky she was to be able to have Peter for a brother, the best brother anyone could possibly have. He always had the time to listen to any little problem, no matter how trivial or insignificant it might appear to someone else, and never let his moods or worries interfere with anyone else's life. He was a real contrast to their sister, Ethel, who seemed impossible to please, and the worst case of a spoiled child anyone had ever seen. She decided not to focus on Ethel now, she wanted nothing to spoil her reunion with Peter.

On the plane ride home, Peter decided it was not the time to mention his love for Cassandra to anyone, except Susan. He was glad she would be picking him up, so they could talk privately.

Peter believed in traveling lightly. After all, Thanksgiving weekend was only four days, and he had plenty of clothes at home in his closet. Coming down the ramp at Logan, he saw Susan waiting for him. She broke out into a huge smile and ran over to the gate and hugged him.

"How's my love bug?" Peter asked, squeezing her tightly.

"Fine, now that you're home," Susan replied gleefully.

Susan was Peter's favorite member of the family; she was three years younger than he, a freshman at Boston University, majoring in art, and a total joy to be around. She had the face of an angel and was always smiling and had a good word for everyone. When she was around, gray clouds had a way of suddenly disappearing in her light. Peter knew she would understand his relationship with Cassandra and could be trusted fully to keep his confidence. On the other hand, his mother, much as he loved her, was the world's biggest yenta, and would have the entire world in their vicinity knowing about his engagement plans at the next Haddassah meeting.

Peter couldn't wait to share the news of his love for Cassandra with Susan, and, as he expected, she was thrilled with the news. He showed her Cassandra's picture and Susan wanted to become a co-conspirator in their romance.

Looking at the picture, Susan said, "Peter, she's simply breathtaking. I'm so happy for you."

"Thanks, I feel lucky to have her."

"*She* is lucky to have you, too, don't forget."

"Do I hear some prejudice there in your voice?"

She smiled, "Sure, but I get a good feeling about her inside.Tell me about her."

Peter proceeded to tell her in detail how they met, about their dates, and his plan to surprise her with an engagement ring from Tiffany's. He was determined to surprise his psychic girlfriend at least once. Susan was simply ecstatic about the engagement, but when he told her Cassandra was Catholic, a red flag went up.

"Peter, you know it doesn't make any difference to me what religion she is. I'll love her like a sister if she makes you happy, but I don't think I'd mention it to Mom and Dad just yet."

"No, you're right, Susan, that's why I am only going to tell you. I'll let them find out gradually."

"Good idea. But I am so excited. Can I go with you to pick out the engagement ring?"

"Of course, who better to help me pick the ring but an artist?"

Thanksgiving was pandemonium at the Brown home, with everyone there from the immediate family and friends dropping over. Peter was jubilant, but he wished he could tell the world of his love. For now though, he was happy he could share his secret with Susan. When everyone remarked on how unusually good he looked, he just thanked them and smiled like the Cheshire cat.

On Long Island, Cassandra was bored to tears. Her holiday was dreadful, just Ryan and Betty and their two children, Bryan and Colleen, two and three, respectively. The food was good, but the festive spirit wasn't with her. She wished in her heart that she were at Peter's side in Boston. She remembered the dream she had had the night before about the faulty exhaust system, and believed she should warn Ryan. During dinner, at what she perceived to be an opportune time, she brought it up.

"Ryan, I had a disturbing dream last night that I'd like to share with you."

"Cassandra, you're just like Nana, with your visions and dreams. "

"Hush, Ryan," Betty said, "let her tell it." She was secretly amused by this Irish mysticism and thought she might gain some interesting tale to amuse her friends.

"Well, I dreamed I was in your large sedan with the windows closed, minding Bryan and Colleen, when we all got drowsy. I started to choke and opened the window, but the children appeared to be unconscious. I sensed immediate danger and I felt it was a warning dream. I also smelled Grandmother's perfume, which is the only reason I'm bringing it up."

"Oh," said Betty, "what does that mean to you?"

"Well, I believe when I smell the perfume it is a message from the other side."

Ryan grabbed his napkin to stifle a laugh, and Cassandra turned crimson. "Well I wish you'd check the exhaust on the car. Better be safe than sorry." Cassandra was annoyed; she felt Ryan saw the whole affair as some amusing joke.

"I'll take the car in tomorrow morning and have it checked if it will make you feel better, Cassandra."

"Suit yourself, Ryan."

"More dessert, Cassandra?" Betty asked in her phony voice.

"No thank you, Betty. Everything was delicious. I'll help you clean up." Cassandra got up from the table and went into the kitchen to help. She was inwardly fuming.

The next morning Ryan stopped by his local gas station on his way to the country club for a golf date with a client.

"Hey Joe, will you check the exhaust?"

"Something wrong,?"

"I don't know, just check it out for me."

"Sure thing, Mr. Colllns. Pull it up here, I'll put it up on the lift."

"Jesus Christ," Joe exclaimed.

"What is it?"

"There's a hole the size of a rat's ass in your exhaust pipe. Good thing you brought it in, you could have suffocated yourself."

"Just fix It," Ryan said, as a chill went down his spine. By God, Cassandra was right after all. He decided not to mention it, though. Betty might be upset.

The weekend separation seemed interminable for both Cassandra and Peter. He called her every night after his parents had gone to bed and they talked for more than an hour. Wait until they get the phone bill, then they'll know something is up, he thought to himself.

The time spent apart erased any doubt about being together. He was determined that nothing and no one, including his parentswould screw up the relationship. They would just have to accept Cassandra. After all, he was the one getting married.

Peter and Susan went downtown to Tiffany's to get the engagement ring. Peter had twelve hundred dollars stashed away, and with it he could get a pretty nice half-carat stone in a beautiful setting. Susan looked at all the rings with him, and they settled on a perfectly cut smaller stone with brilliance to make up for its small size.

"Oh, Peter, it's just beautiful."

"Do you think it's too small, Sis?"

"Oh, no, its lovely. The setting makes an elegant statement and besides, it's a perfect stone. "

"You're right. I'm sure she'll love it."

Peter paid for the ring, and smuggled it into the house in Susan's oversized shopping bag. When his mother asked them where they had been, Susan covered for him, saying she had wanted him to see some ice skates she was planning to get, and to buy some Chanukah gifts early. The explanation satisfied his mother. She was pleased that her children were close and got along so well. Her other daughter, Ethel, the middle child, was not blessed with Peter's looks or brains, and wasn't the sweetest child to raise. Ethel, a junior at Boston Universlty, lived at home, wore glasses and had a bad case of acne. Ethel and Peter didn't get along so she was happy that Susan at least was there as the peacemaker of the family.

Susan got along with Ethel and was the mediator in all family disputes. Her mother smiled looking at her, knowing what a wonderful wife and mother Susan would make. Susan was always after Peter to bring his friends home and introduce them to her, but he felt that at seventeen she was too young and, besides, she would meet plenty of young men in college. Susan just smiled. She was always asked out on dates and went, all the boys loved her, but she couldn't settle on any one in particular. She was like Peter in that respect, or like he was, until he met Cassandra. Susan was happy to see him head over heels in love because it made her believe maybe it would happen to her, too.

Peter had to see Cassandra when he flew back Sunday night. He wanted to surprise her with the ring, not being able to wait until their Monday night study-date. When he rang up to her room from the desk at Trinity College he found she hadn't arrived yet, and drove out to the airport to pick her up. She was delayed an hour in the air from New York and when she got off the plane was overjoyed to see him waiting at the gate. She had felt he'd be there waiting, but pretended instead to be surprised.

"Darling!" he rushed and hugged her, sweeping her off the ground. They kissed and hugged, oblivious to the onlookers and other deplaning passengers.

"Peter, I'm so glad to see you," she said, starting to relax. She had been under incredible strain since the dream. "Let's get something to eat. It seems like light years since we've seen each other."

"I know. I have a better idea. Let's go to a motel for the night. I'll take you back to school early tomorrow morning. You can say you missed the flight tonight and arrive back tomorrow morning."

Cassandra liked the idea. "Fine. I don't ever want to be apart from you again."

He picked up her luggage at the baggage claim and they headed down the road to the Holiday Inn. The same clerk was on duty who had been there the previous week, and he gave them the same room. They ordered room service and, when it arrived, Peter slipped the little blue Tiffany box onto the tray. Cassandra saw it and instantly knew what was inside.

"Open it," Peter said.

"No. You open it."

Peter opened the box and placed the ring on her finger. The tears poured down her face as she looked, transfixed, at the sparkling diamond.

"Peter, it's the most beautiful thing I have ever seen in my life. "

"Not as beautiful as you."

Looking into his eyes, she realized that their love was real and her fears were groundless. They embraced, ignoring dinner, preferring a night of love.

Chapter Twelve

There were only three weeks between Thanksgiving and winter recess. Peter intended to fill them with joy for both himself and Cassandra. He would tell his family about her over the holidays and introduce her to them for New Year's. Yes, he was going to make certain the next few weeks were filled with happiness. Cassandra and Peter, when they weren't in class, or he wasn't in a lab or at basketball practice, spent every spare minute together. Each weekend they signed out, and spent Friday night to Monday morning at a nearby motel. Their life was idyllic.

Peter's parents made him a present each year of a subscription to the Lane Series, a program of ballet, opera, major classical and popular artists, and road tours of Broadway shows, opportunities that would otherwise be denied to the residents of Vermont. It was a cultural bonanza, and when not studying for exams or playing basketball, Peter always availed himself of every event. Now that he and Cassandra were engaged, they went together. It was wonderful that music and theatre were loves of Cassandra's, too. Having so much in common made their relationship even closer and more special. In addition to being an accomplished athlete, Peter was a deep thinker, and Cassandra loved spending hours discussing philosophy and current events, listening to his acute political insights.

Peter loved Cassandra's. Until meeting her, he had never encountered a girl who could keep up with him intellectually. Because of her innate brightness and Sarah's training, Cassandra was a source of unending joy for Peter. Cassandra vowed she would never become a boring housewife like her sister-in-law, Betty. No, she would never let her mind slip to the level of only being able to discuss mundane affairs. Her grandmother taught her that men eventually became bored with wives who let their minds and appearances go. Cassandra wanted always to be beautiful and intriguing, and she reminded herself of her goals daily.

For all the education Cassandra received from her grandmother, there was one gaping omission. Her grandmother, having the traditional Irish reticence concerning sex, had never once broached the subject of birth control to her beloved granddaughter. Sarah had just assumed Cassandra would wait until marriage before indulging in what she termed "the marital act." However, Cassandra took after Sarah's own less conventional mother, Esther Cullen, not only in her psychic gift, but in her more unconventional morality. It never occurred to Cassandra to wait until after marriage to sleep with Peter, not with at least six more years of schooling ahead of her. She was in love, and in her eyes that made everything fine.

Elaine was beginning to get on Cassandra's nerves. Several times there had been sharp words between them about little matters. Elaine was jealous of Cassandra's relationship with Peter, and when she saw the diamond engagement ring, she almost turned green with envy. Elaine's only topics of conversation were gleaned from the articles she read in magazines, which were aimed largely at sex-crazed adolescents. But to the girls in school, Elaine was the expert on the subject of birth control. One afternoon Cassandra decided to ask her opinion on the matter.

Elaine believed the pill to be the only really safe method of birth control, the one that was infallible, although one needed an appointment to be examined and get a prescription. But, with Cassandra's family history of strokes, it would be highly doubtful that a doctor would ever prescribe it .

"Cassandra, I think you should see a good

gynecologist and seek his advice. If you are contemplating having sex, seek an expert opinion."

Cassandra thought Elaine was being a bitch, merely trying to get her to admit she was sleeping with Peter. Seeing no visible reaction to her statement, Elaine decided to push a little further. "I hope you have enough sense not to sleep with someone if you're not using anything. I mean, Vatican Roulette has ruined many a girl's future."

"Thanks for your concern, Elaine. I'll let you know when I need it."

"Better safe than sorry, I always say."

Cassandra hadn't been feeling at all well since Thanksgiving, and was concerned. She thought it might be the flu, but that was weeks ago and no flu lasted four weeks. Although she was frightened, she wanted to find out what was going on in her body. Cassandra hated going to the gynecologist. She was very private and did not like anyone poking around in her private parts. But when she was late with her period, which had only happened once before, during the loss of her grandmother, she decided to get checked out.

She almost passed out when the doctor said he believed she was pregnant. Oh my God, what would she do? Of course she would never have an abortion. She and Peter would just get married. She hated that it had happened this way, but she loved him and wanted to spend the rest of her life with him, so maybe, as her grandmother would say, this was the hand of God. She would tell him when she knew for certain and take the consequences. Until then, she would tell no one, especially Elaine, but inside she was certain she was carrying Peter's child and she alternated between elation and depression.

The results were positive: the baby was due in late August. She appeared to be in perfect health, and the doctor felt sure that everything would proceed smoothly. He made an appointment for the next week for a session with a nutritionist and suggested several books for her and her husband to read. Her husband. If he only knew. She would have to share this news with Peter and it couldn't wait. She thought, God, was there ever a good time to have a baby?

As the fates would have it, it was the night of the full moon, and, if it were possible, pregnancy made Cassandra look even more beautiful. She gazed at her engagement ring and was full of hope for Peter's joy at the arrival of their little girl, Catherine, who would be born about the time of her grandmother's birthday, she would be a little Leo.

Peter picked Cassandra up as usual, they went for a bite to eat and planned to study together at the library. At dinner, Peter noticed Cassandra was unusally quiet.

"You look like the cat that swallowed the canary. What's up?"

"I'm pregnant."

"You're kidding."

"No, Peter, I'm not. You're going to be a father."

Peter flushed, "Cassandra, how could you do this to us? You must be crazy!"

The words struck out at her like a knife deep in her heart. Tears came to her eyes. "Peter, It happened on our first night together."

"Holy God." He was fuming. An animal anger raged inside of him. "We'll just have to see a doctor. Larry's girlfriend went to him, and she's fine."

"What do you mean?"

"An abortion. I mean we just can't have a child now."

Cassandra stared and quietly got up. "Take me back to the dorm."

"I'll be glad to."

Cassandra and Peter didn't speak until they got back to the dorm.

"Can I call you tomorrow?" Peter asked.

"Yes." Cassandra didn't wait for him to open the door for her; she let herself out and slammed the door, not looking back.

Her heart was breaking, the joy she felt over the advent of their child washed away by her first tears since she had met Peter. She decided to have a good soak in the tub, it would help. There was no way she would abort her child, their child. She loved Peter and she loved the baby growing inside of her, she would have it and take the consequences. She was healthy, and rich, and she was sure he'd change his mind. After all, he loved her, didn't he? Of course he'd change his mind, it was just the shock.

Peter was livid. He stormed back to the dorm. Ed looked up as Peter unlocked the door and threw his books on the bed.

"What's eating you?"

"Cassandra's pregnant."

"Jesus, what rotten luck. What'll you do?"

" I want her to get rid of it, that's the right thing to do, but she wants it."

"Lord."

"I know."

"When she thinks of the reality of it she'll change her mind."

"I hope you're right."

"Hey, let's have a few beers, you'll feel better."

"Sounds like a good idea." Peter put his hand out on the window sill and popped open a cool beer. His head was swimming. He a would sleep on it then he'd know what to do.

Meanwhile, back in her dorm room, Cassandra sobbed herself to sleep.

Chapter Thirteen

The next morning Peter awoke with a terrific headache. He had a roaring hangover, and he felt awful. He never abused alcohol, but last night, after learning of Cassandra's pregnancy, he felt he'd had a reason to get drunk. Only it seemed somehow worse this morning. Upon waking, he was not only about to be a father, but hung-over, and not feeling good about the baby or himself. He didn't want to see Cassandra in this condition, yet had to talk to her. They just couldn't have a baby now, it was simply out of the question; she would have to understand.

An abortion wasn't the end of the world, he would make her understand. It was her damn Catholic upbringing, that's all. The Irish loved to breed, and children were more sacred to them than anything else, he'd always heard. He'd talk some sense into her and erase some of the tribal myths that were enslaving her. Yes, he would see to that.

He decided on calling her instead of seeing her in person, so he telephoned the dorm and waited for her to come to the phone.

"Hello."

"Cassandra, it's Peter. How are you?"

"Fine, I guess. How are you?"

"Cassandra, I feel bad about the way I reacted last night when you told me you were pregnant."

"Peter, I wish we could discuss this in private, I hate talking about this on the hall phone."

"Cassandra, I can't see you today. Listen to me, I love you very much, but having this child is simply madness. If you insist on having it, go ahead, but don't expect me to be a part of it. I was tricked."

"You weren't tricked. I didn't plan this child. I love you Peter, it's our child, I couldn't abort it."

"Cassandra, I love you but I won't go along with this scheme."

"It's not a scheme. When two people love each other they get married."

"Get real, Cassandra, it's not on my agenda yet. I love you, after all, we're engaged. I figured we'd get married in four years when I graduate from med school."

"I'm sorry I've upset your agenda, Peter."

"I'm sorry, too." He paused. "Cassandra, getting married now is the stupidest idea I've ever heard."

Cassandra didn't hear him. She was reeling from shock.

"Are you all right?"

"Yes, I'm fine," she was crying.

"I'll leave you alone. Talk to you later." He hung up.

A week passed and Cassandra didn't hear from him. In the meantime, she didn't change her mind. She decided she would leave school and start a new life in New York with their child. She wouldn't tell anyone until it was too late to have an abortion. She wanted this child, she wouldn't go through life alone, and she couldn't kill the child, the proof of Peter's love for her. She sounded like a romantic, but what the hell, she was, and she couldn't get rid of it. Besides, she liked the idea of life growing inside her. Baby Catherine. She would survive, the Collins women were strong, Grandmother always said so. She would show Peter. She'd have the child .

She couldn't believe Peter wouldn't call, after all they were still engaged. She looked at the beautiful solitaire on her finger. Why was he punishing her so? What had she done? After all, he was the father, why wasn't he happy? It couldn't be the money, his family was wealthy and Cassandra's allowance was more than most people with families earned after years in a good job. Maybe it was the responsibility, or the shock of it all . . .

The following week a group of the girls went down to Lake Champlain to ice skate. Cassandra wasn't good at it, but she wanted the fresh air and exercise, and besides, she was only in her second month. They were all out on the ice when Elaine and the others started racing. Cassandra started out with them. Her foot caught on a ridge of twisted ice, throwing her through the air, crashing down into a snow bank. The impact was great and she lost consciousness for a moment. When she came to, she realized she was bleeding and asked Elaine to rush her to the hospital.

The doctor in the emergency room realized upon examining her what was happening; in order to stop the hemorrhaging, he'd have to take the baby.

Cassandra was shaking at the prospect, and as she was wheeled into surgery under sedation, kept calling out Peter's name. Elaine knew what was happening, but never called Peter. In her jealous heart she was glad to see "Miss Goody Two Shoes" suffer.

Chapter Fourteen

Later that evening Elaine felt she should go over to the hospital to check on Cassandra. She went up to the maternity ward and quietly let herself into the ugly green room. Cassandra was sleeping lightly; she was under sedation and would be in the hospital for about three days. The school was aware that she was being hospitalized for an ovarian cyst, nothing more.

Elaine had seen to that much but, inside, she was secretly happy that some misfortune had befallen Cassandra. After all, why should she be the only one with such rotten luck? All the discussions in the world in religion class about Karma, the law of balance, was bullshit as far as she was concerned; some people had good luck, and some had bad luck and that was all there was to it.

Elaine filed her nails, waiting impatiently for Cassandra to open her eyes. Cassandra began to stir.

"Are you all right, Cassandra? It's me, Elaine."

"Where is Peter? I dreamed that he came to take me out of here." Cassandra was very doped up from the medication.

"Honey, I don't things you'll ever hear from that louse again. Don't worry about him, as I always say—there's too many fish in the sea."

Cassandra turned her head and began

to cry softly into the pillow. Elaine was uncomfortable and was sorry she came.

"Is there anything I can do for you?"

Cassandra shook her head.

"I'll check on you tomorrow. See you later."

Cassandra motioned goodbye with her hand. Inside she was tormented; where was Peter and why was this happening to her? If only Sarah were here, she'd know the answers. Once again she began to feel alone, and lay in limbo staring at the ceiling.

The day after Cassandra lost the baby, Peter walked over to Trinity College from his dorm room at the university. The snow was falling and everything would be all right. After all, he was shocked about the news that Cassandra was pregnant. How could he have made such a stupid mistake? He just assumed she was on the pill like all the other girls he had bedded.

That was just it: Cassandra was not like all the other girls. She was special, different, more beautiful, more ethereal, and he was hopelessly in love with her. He would risk it all for her, and somehow he felt it would be worth it. A lot of guys go through med school with a wife and kid. He could do it. He'd turn down the European vacation his parents had promised him for a graduation present. Instead he'd take the cash and buy a condo in Burlington for Cassandra and the baby.

Inside, he was a bundle of confusion. The idea of becoming a father seemed totally absurd and at the same time thrilled him beyond his wildest imagination. A child, a new life in the Brown family. He hoped it would be a son, the pride of a man who had impregnated his love burst through. Yes, Ed was right—it would be fine. Somehow arrival of a baby would make his parents forget that Cassandra wasn't Jewish. How could they resist his firstborn, their grandchild? Yes, it would be fine.

When he stopped at the reception desk, the Sister on duty looked up from her newspaper.

"Yes, may I help you, young man?"

He smiled at the Sister, thinking, "I just knocked up one of your young ladies."

"Yes, Cassandra Collins please."

"Is she expecting you?"

"No."

"Well, I'll ring up and see if she is in her room."

Elaine answered the hall phone. "Yes."

"A caller for Cassandra Collins."

"She's not here, Sister. Who is it?"

"I'll let you talk to him. Young man," she said handing him the receiver. Peter smiled.

"Hello?" Elaine said.

"Oh, Elaine, it's Peter. Is Cassandra in?"

"I'm afraid not, Peter."

"Do you know where she is?"

"No I don't, Peter." Elaine said, lying.

"I've got to talk to her, and I have a 4:30 flight out of Boston today."

"Well, I don't know when to expect her back, Peter."

"Well, I have a letter for her, I'll leave it here at the desk.

Tell her I dropped by, O.K.?"

"Certainly Peter, I'll make sure and do that. Good-bye."

Elaine hung the receiver up and put on her shoes. "That bastard, I wonder what he wrote to Miss Lonelyhearts."

She left the room and went downstairs to get the letter Peter left for Cassandra, brought it back upstairs and opened it.

Sunday

Dear Cassandra.

What can I say? I'm sorry about what I said, and how I reacted when you told me of the baby. It must have sounded totally insensitive and uncaring on my part. I am begging your forgiveness.

I want you in my life, I love you and know we will find a way to make it work out somehow. The baby was created out of love, and I had no right to ask you to abort it. Let's put this argument behind us, and get married. I know my family will come through for us after we are married. Somehow babies seem to make things right. Call me at home.

All my love,
Peter
OXOXOXO

After reading the letter, Elaine picked up the trash can next to the desk and dropped the letter in with the empty Coke cans, candy wrappers and cigarette butts.

As she opened the incinerator door she unemotionally watched Cassandra's future go down the chute with the other trash. As she returned to her room and flopped down on the bed to read her latest issue of *Cosmopolitan*, she removed the incident from her mind.

Cassandra was weak after getting out of the hospital. She had lost a great deal of blood after the miscarriage and was still in emotional shock from not hearing from Peter during her three day ordeal. Little did she know he was in great pain too, and the letter, which was meant to heal their wounds, was now ashes scattered at the bottom of an incinerator in Trinity's dorm.

Arriving back at the dorm, Cassandra was surprised to see Elaine packing her things.

"Where are you going?"

Elaine answered, "Beats the hell out of me. If you're so psychic, you should be able to tell me." Elaine threw a suitcase around. "I had a little party in the room while you were recovering, and the hall proctor caught me. I've been given the boot."

Cassandra wasn't surprised. As she sat down on her bed, she saw the little world she had constructed beginning to collapse. There was no way that she could continue in school with the trauma she had been through. Even though she was a straight A student, she figured, "What do I need with a B.A. in liberal arts anyway?" She would rather get on with developing her psychic gifts, and get on with her life.

She had no business remaining in school with the other students. Here, at 19, she was a woman who had already experienced a passion some women go their whole life without knowing, conceived her lover's child, and by some cruel twist of fate, lost both her lover and her child. The memories of Peter were too painful to be borne alone in Burlington, and she needed desperately to heal herself. The madness and excitement of a large city were the medicines she needed to make her forget Peter and go on with her life. Cassandra tuned psychically into Elaine's thoughts, "You are moving to New York."

Elaine turned around, startled . "You really are psychic aren't you? I'm going to check into a Manhattan hotel and look for an apartment. Then I'll get a job on an airline, and hopefully enroll in an acting class." Elaine took a drag off her cigarette. Cassandra asked her for one.

"Mind if I bum one of your cigarettes?"

"Not at all, didn't know you smoked."

"I do now."

Cassandra lit up and inhaled, feeling the smoke enter her lungs. Cassandra thought quickly. She knew in her heart that Elaine was a materialistic bitch who was going to turn the expulsion from school into a launching pad for her new life, the one she had wanted all along. Cassandra thought she should follow suit. Move to New York with her and get on with her life. Although she was by nature a calm, peaceful person, she wanted her life to amount to something. Had she carried the baby, Peter's baby, to term, she would have been a great mother, but she also wanted her life to make a difference in the world. She wanted to know herself better, and learn to use her clairvoyance to enrich her life and the lives of others.

Out of the grief and shock, some little voice inside of her head rallied, screaming "New York City here I come." She asked Elaine, "Would you like to continue as roommates?"

Elaine was surprised. "Why not?"

She knew Cassandra had the bucks, and even though she didn't like her, she figured, in her opportunistic mind, what the hell? So, not unlike her grandmother and great grandmother before her, Cassandra set off for the big city with faith in herself and her ability to succeed intact. She opened her closets and started packing. She would write to the registrar, explaining her withdrawal. In the meantime, she would move in with Elaine and then jet off to the Caribbean for two weeks and soak up some sun. Then she would enroll in psychic development classes.

She took off the diamond ring for the first time since Peter had placed it there, put it in the silver Tiffany baby cup on the shelf, and took another drag on the cigarette.

Chapter Fifteen

During the holidays, Peter couldn't believe how the phone didn't ring for him, day after day. His sister, Susan, was worried about his moods—so unlike Peter, especially around the holidays, when he was usually so "up", seeing old high school chums and busy exchanging stories around the table with the family. Now, instead of participating he would sequester himself in his room, seldom leaving except for meals and attendance at "required" family events, where he weakly smiled, appearing to be in a world of his own making.

Susan was the one person who could make Peter laugh. He always had a special place in his heart for his little sister, but even she was unable to bring the sparkle back into his eyes. After a week of this behavior, Susan knocked on Peter's door.

"Yeah," Peter answered lethargically.

"Peter, it's Susan. Can I come in?"

"Sure, Sis. Come on in."

Peter opened the door, he hadn't made his bed in a week and there were soda cans and dirty dishes lying around on the floor.

"Excuse the mess, I haven't been feeling myself lately."

"So I've noticed. What's wrong Peter? I mean something really terrible must have happened to make you feel this way."

Tears welled up in Peter's eyes. "Cassandra and I aren't seeing each other anymore."

"That's terrible, Peter. Is there a reason?"

Peter broke down, sobbing, and told Susan the whole story; with each word she felt his pain and knew more surely how much her brother loved Cassandra, and how devastated he was at her seeming lack of concern for him. After hearing the whole story, Susan asked. "Are you sure she received the letter?"

"Yes, I'm sure."

"Then I don't understand why she didn't at least call."

"I can't figure it out either."

"What will you do, Peter?"

"What can I do? Burlington is a small town, I'll most likely run into her."

"I'm certain you two will get back together. Love conquers all, and all that."

"We'll see."

Susan let herself out of the room. "Goodnight, Peter. See you in the morning."

"Goodnight, Sis, and thanks."

As she shut the door, and made her way down the hall, she heard him crying softly into his pillow. Not since he was a little boy had he cried himself to sleep.

January in Vermont is bleak especially if you are not a skier. It was a cloudy, gray day when Peter arrived back on campus. Ed had already returned from the holidays and was busy at work on a project for his senior thesis, when Peter came into the room.

"Hey, pal. Happy New Year!"

"Thanks a lot." Peter said dejectedly. "I hope this year is better than last year."

From the look on his face, Ed knew that Peter hadn't heard from Cassandra over the holidays.

"She didn't call, Peter?"

"No way. Guess I've really been shot down. Can't figure it out either. "

"I'd go over to Trinity and check it out. After all, a two week vacation can really smooth things over."

"Maybe you're right. I'll go on over after I unpack."

"How was your vacation, Ed?"

Ed proceeded to tell Peter all about his super holiday at home with his family and friends while Peter unpacked.

It began snowing as Peter walked over to Trinity with hope in his heart. He thought to himself, after all she did keep the ring. He felt that was a good sign. When he arrived at Trinity, he asked the nun at the desk for the phone. Peter asked for Cassandra, but was told she had dropped out of school. In disbelief, he asked the nun at the desk where she was and he was informed that she had not enrolled for the semester. Leaving the dorm, he felt lower than he had ever been in his life.

In the three weeks he had grieved over the apparent breakup, he never once believed the separation would be permanent. It had never occurred to him that "no" was also a possible answer.

He vowed he would never again experience the pain he was going through. He would never fall in love again. He would devote himself to his career, and bury his feelings deep inside himself, so he would be safe from the hurt and failure of his love for Cassandra.

He turned away from Trinity and walked up the hill. The falling snow covered the tracks behind him.

BOOK TWO

Chapter Sixteen

Christmas week seemed a grotesque parody of Shakespeare's *Twelfth Night* for Cassandra. She felt like Olivia, first in a foreign land comprised of brothers, sister-in-laws, nieces, nephews, and distant relations, all the while being forced by circumstances to pretend everything was fine.

This was the first Christmas without her grandmother and, combined with the breakup with Peter and the miscarriage, she felt alienated and alone. The contrast of her grieving state to the happiness of her brothers and their families made her understand why so many lonely souls commit suicide at Christmas. To complicate matters, she developed a severe cold, adding to her already confused state. Although the cold gave her an excuse for acting slightly off-center, she felt like her psyche was shot-up with Demarol, allowing numbness to replace any positive emotions she might have had because of the holiday.

As bad as the days were the nights

were worse. Then, she was at the mercy of her unconscious mind. When she managed to obliterate everything in sleep she had a recurring nightmare: she and Peter were living in a large house somewhere in the country. The dream suddenly switched to an airport where she and Peter were sitting holding their beautiful baby daughter, Catherine. An announcement is made over the intercom, and Cassandra must get up and leave immediately. She boards the plane, only to realize she has left Peter and the baby behind her. As she turns around she sees Peter crying, holding the baby up, waving good-bye. She begins crying, as she is ushered into her seat by a bald pilot, who explains to her not to be upset, the separation is only temporary. Cassandra looks into her handbag and searches frantically for a return ticket, but before she has a chance to find it, she awakens in a cold sweat, feeling betrayed and abandoned.

On the morning of New Year's day, Tom drove Cassandra to Kennedy airport where she boarded a jet for a month of healing in St. Croix. During her early years it was a family ritual that each year after Christmas Sarah would pack herself and the grandchildren off to her favorite Caribbean island for what she called "two weeks of heaven". The family would check into the Club Commanche, a large friendly inn in the heart of Christianstead, where they spent some of their happiest times together. They loved the hotel; with its large rooms which overlooked the beautiful harbor, the walled salt water pool bordered by stately palm trees, and the fabulous fresh seafood restaurant. Sarah loved the gregarious international clientele, and the children loved the warm, sunny weather. The Collins' yearly forays broke up when the twins married, and started new traditions. So it was with great hope of recapturing joyful memories that Cassandra fled to the security of the past, a past far away from her uncertain present.

The first morning of her vacation, dressed in a lovely white cotton sun-dress and wearing an oversized floppy straw hat, Cassandra sat at the pool, and decided to use the month in St. Croix to whip her body into shape by doing forty laps each morning in the pool, followed by a twenty minute meditation to keep her mind on an even keel.

Every morning, after meditation and laps in the pool, while the sun still wasn't too strong for her fair skin, Cassandra would take a walk around Christianstead and go down to the dock strip to pick up a morning paper. She would return to the hotel to breakfast with the hotel patrons and locals who gathered every morning to eat, drink coffee and discuss the news of the day.

The restaurant was situated on the second floor of the hotel, with an enormous balcony that let you look down at the street below and see the whole world pass in front of your eyes, while you lingered over your cup of coffee and cigarette. The locals sprinkled sugar on the bannister of the porch, and goldfinches would fly off the trees to eat, and sing in appreciation before flying away.

The food was incredibly good, and Cassandra loved the fresh melon and hot pancakes. She stuck to decaffeinated coffee, so she wouldn't have any anxiety attacks. She loved the people who gathered every day for breakfast. It was a democratic society composed of wealthy tourists from Europe and New York, disaffected workers from the mainland, who came seeking paradise and stayed year after year, and, finally, people, like herself, who just wanted to get away from it all.

While she was staying at the hotel a film crew from a prime time television show was filming two episodes on the island, so she got to meet some Los Angeles characters with the show. One cameraman asked her to be an extra in one of the scenes they were shooting that day and Cassandra agreed for the fun of it.

Cassandra brought her set of watercolors from home, to paint some of St. Croix's natural beauty spots, which were unspoiled, not like so many of the other "tourist traps." Cassandra found no difficulty in finding beautiful views to paint. She felt a magical link to this island, discovered the day before her birthday, almost five hundred years before. Somehow, St. Croix managed to retain its sense of harmony, and Cassandra hoped that here she would be able to regain hers.

In the afternoons Cassandra rented a car and took long drives around the picturesque island. When she saw something she wanted to capture in paint, she would stop and sketch it. Sometimes she would sit and take out her watercolors and paint the picture on the spot, or, if she was restless, take out her Nikkon camera and shoot the scene from different angles, so she could use it as a guide for painting later when she returned to the hotel.

Cassandra didn't feel alone at the Commanche. There were several of Sarah's friends who knew her from years before when she frequented the resort with her family. They were a friendly group of older people who looked upon her either as a daughter or godchild to be doted upon. She simply loved the attention she received. Because it was not a singles resort, she had no unwelcome or unsettling propositions to upset her delicate balance.

In the evenings, she would sit out on the big patio with the other travelers, looking out over the peaceful harbor, and listening to the steel drum bands from across the Island on the Bay. St. Croix proved to be the healing elixir Cassandra needed to bring her away from the emotional abyss of life without Peter.

The week before returning to New York Cassandra began to gather her thoughts. She needed an apartment. In Vermont, she had wanted to move with Elaine, but now she changed her mind. Every time she visualized Elaine, she perceived a black cloud around her head, boding ill for her future. Elaine would definitely not be part of Cassandra's future in New York. She didn't want negative aspects of her past clinging to her.

Cassandra had had the foresight, when her grandmother died, to store her furniture, rather than auction it off, as the twins wanted to do. There were several pieces she would love to have for her own apartment. Furnishing a New York apartment the right way was quite different from decorating a dorm room at Trinity.

She decided to look up her grandmother's old friend and confidant Danny Darcello to help. She would keep the large black baby-grand piano and the exquisite Chinese Chippendale dining room suite, but she would want to furnish her living room and bedroom with new things, and mix them with some of the better antiques to have the feeling of a French salon. She would look for an apartment in a good building around Sutton Place, and buy it. No sense renting when you had the money she had, so her mind was made up.

She would call Elaine and let her know of her plans when she returned from St. Croix.

The four weeks spent in St. Croix worked wonders. Her body was exquisite once again, her morale back in winning form and, except for the occasional nightmare, her mind was clear. She was proud of the watercolors she created while on the island. Three were so fine that she would have them framed upon her return to New York. One was a sunset with a sugar mill against the pink sky on the north shore of the island. The second was an afternoon scene of Fredrikstead, with the local people talking on the steps of a Victorian homestead. The third, her favorite, was a sunrise over the water, symbolic of the new dawn she felt coming into her life.

Before she left the island Cassandra went into her favorite shop on the island, Little Switzerland, and bought a small crystal swan. From the time she was a girl, each year, her grandmother would buy her a piece of crystal, an animal, or bauble to hang in her window, and this year, being the first year she wasn't presented with one, she bought one for herself.

She also bought a Cartier lighter, a Lalique ashtray, and a beautiful cigarette-case for her new habit. She absolutely hated the way the girls in school would light up with cheap disposable lighters, and flick their ashes into empty soda cans. If she was going to smoke she vowed she would do it with style. She loved the taste of tobacco and its aroma, and she was fascinated by fire. She figured, if that was her major vice, she wasn't doing so badly after all.

Flying into JFK after a month in the sun-drenched Caribbean, Cassandra was stunned by the cold, snow-covered vista. From the air, the city had an unreal look, similar to the moonscape she had seen in the space pavilion, the year before, at the World's Fair. The sky was a clear, icy blue, and the skyline of New York was utterly magnificent, shining in the noonday sun, sparkling with the new-fallen snow from the previous night's flurries.

The broken little girl who had gone to the islands to heal, was now returning a woman. A woman with her mind made up, determined and confident.

She possessed beauty, talent, and sincerity, an unbeatable combination for taking the city by storm. Cassandra was serene, knowing she was coming home to her city, where she was born 19 years before. Now its daughter was returning home for her inheritance.

She decided not to call her brothers to pick her up at the airport like she'd promised. Instead she ordered a limousine and directed the driver to take her to the Plaza Hotel. She was going to begin her life in New York on the best possible note, and the Plaza symbolized the finest Manhattan had to offer.

Chapter Seventeen

Cassandra had several important calls to make before settling down in her suite overlooking Central Park. She made a courtesy call to Tom to let him know her number. He was busy, as usual, so his secretary took the call. She told the secretary to leave the identical message for Ryan, and not to have either of them call her until tomorrow morning.

She wasn't going to be wasting time looking for a place to live, either. She had to make an immediate appointment with Danny Darcello to find an apartment and get things underway. Even though her income was over four thousand dollars a month, it was costing almost that much to stay at the Plaza for four weeks and Cassandra was determined not to rough it in New York. She called the operator to get Danny's number, then dialed. The phone rang, and his secretary answered.

"Hello. Darcello's Shop of Interior Design.' The voice was very polite, but cold.

"Yes, this is Cassandra Collins, Sarah Cullen Collins' granddaughter. May I please speak to Mr. Darcello?"

"He is busy with a client right now. May I have your number? I'll have him return the call."

Cassandra left the number of the hotel. She barely had time to put the phone down when it rang.

"Hello."

"Cassandra, this is Danny. How are you, dear?"

"Fine, Danny. Thank you for calling me back so soon."

"How can I help you, darling?"

"I'd like to get together with you and talk, Danny. I've dropped out of school and I need to find a place in New York to live. I'd like you to help me fix it up when I find it."

"No problem at all, dear. How about lunch tomorrow and we'll talk?"

"Great. Thanks so much."

"Come by the shop, on First and Fifty-third about 11:30. O.K.?

"See you then."

As she hung up, Cassandra felt good, Danny would help her get settled so she wouldn't have to worry.

The next call was to Elaine in Connecticut. Cassandra dreaded this call, but she needed to get it over with. Elaine's mother answered.

"Hello, Mrs. Martin. This is Cassandra, Elaine's former roommate. May I please speak to Elaine?"

"Cassandra. Elaine has moved into Manhattan with Colleen, her friend from high school. Let me give you her number."

She gave Cassandra the number and they exchanged pleasantries. When Cassandra got off the phone, she was at once relieved and annoyed. Glad Elaine found a place to live, she was irritated to be left out.

It is funny, she thought, how you can

be happy and annoyed at the same time. She rang Elaine, who answered.

"Hi, Cassandra. Where are you?"

"I'm in. New York, staying at the Plaza."

"Gee, that's terrific. I guess my Mom told you I got an apartment here in the city."

"Yes, and thanks for including me."

"Don't be upset with me, Cassandra. It just came up and I grabbed it. You know, opportunity knocking, and all that crap. Anyway I couldn't manage to stay home with the folks. It was murder there."

"Oh, I understand."

"Well, come down and see us. I'm living with my best friend from high school, Colleen. She's a stewardess with Eastern Airlines, and we've got a great place down here at Peter Cooper Village."

"Where is that, Elaine?

"It's on 23rd Street and FDR Drive. The apartment is a huge two bedroom, two baths. My father got it for us, and the best part is, it's only $550 a month."

Elaine gave Cassandra the address and Cassandra promised to visit her, as soon as she was settled.

Elaine went on to inform Cassandra that, after a month of going around to all the modeling agencies with her head shots and portfolio, she was throwing in the towel, and getting a job with Colleen at the airline. Cassandra listened to her plans, and thought to herself, it sounds like Elaine, the realist, running true to form. When the going got rough, Elaine bailed out. She always figured the best way to profit from any situation.

Cassandra mentally stored the information, realizing the Elaines of this world are a dime-a-dozen, but they are also the survivors, finding their niche and clinging to it. Now to find the right teacher. She remembered seeing a column in the *Village Voice* with advertisements for psychic development classes.

She put on her white fox jacket and ran downstairs for a copy of the latest *Voice* and to grab a sandwich at the Palm Court. Cassandra sat down at the table, and the waitress took her order. She ordered a chunky chicken salad sandwich on pumpernickel bread, her favorite, with a whiskey sour to celebrate her arrival back to New York. While the order was being prepared, Cassandra remained oblivious to the beautiful surroundings, with the lovely violins and piano playing in the background.

She eagerly flipped the pages of the paper, finally locating the column for psychic development classes. There it was under the heading *Body, Mind, and Spirit.* She scanned the column expectantly, letting her finger run down the column of advertisers. She stopped at an ad that was in block form. It read, *Mind Dynamics: Unlock Your Inner Psychic Potential.* It was listed at a good address on Fifth Avenue, and gave free introductory lectures on Wednesday evenings. Cassandra decided she would attend the lecture later in the week and investigate its possibilities.

The morning of her luncheon appointment with Danny Darcello, Cassandra decided to walk over to his interior decorating shop on First and Fifty-third. It was a beautiful day, the sun was shining, and the snow was beginning to melt.

Cassandra could feel high energy in the air, quite a contrast to the relaxed vibrations of St. Croix. Everyone in New York City seemed to be operating on speed. No wonder there were so many shrinks, analysts, and astrologers on this island, the people needed someone to take the time to listen. Since her grandmother's death, apart from Peter, there seemed no one to listen to Cassandra's problems.

It was nice of Danny to invite her to lunch. He had come out to the house on Long Island, two or three times a year to visit with her grandmother. Sarah always told her: if you are ever in trouble, call on Danny. He was her grandmother's best friend. Sarah had had many acquaintances over the years, people she loved and helped, but Danny was the person she relied on, the one who never let her down. Cassandra hoped he would help her in the same way.

Danny was now in his early sixties, an extremely handsome gentleman, always dressed in well-tailored three piece suits, with a few exquisite pieces of jewelry. His being obviously gay was totally accepted by Sarah, as well as by Cassandra. Danny had a long-standing relationship with Donald, a younger advertising executive, with whom he had lived for twenty years. Everywhere they were accepted as a couple. Cassandra lovingly referred to Danny as her "fairy godfather".

Danny was waiting for Cassandra, as she walked up to his shop. She was right on time. As she entered via the big glass door, he jumped up and hugged her.

"Darling, how are you?" he said smiling.

"Great, Danny." Cassandra kissed him. "Good to see you."

Cassandra was genuinely glad to see him, and he knew it.

"I haven't seen you since your grandmother's funeral. You certainly look wonderful."

"Thank you, so do you."

Danny studied her for a minute, "You are not wearing your glasses. I knew something was different."

Cassandra laughed, "I'm a regular vamp now, aren't I?"

"You said it, not me", Danny laughed. "I hope you're hungry. I made reservations at the Russian Tea Room for twelve thirty; let's walk over."

Danny put on a beautiful dark ranch mink coat, and they walked over to the restaurant on Fifty-seventh Street arm-in-arm.

"So, how's your love life, Cassandra? A pretty girl like you must have plenty of boyfriends."

"Oh, I'm not involved right now." Cassandra replied quietly. Danny was quite psychic himself.

"Well, I'll not press the issue, but if you'd like to talk about it, I'll be happy to listen."

"Well, you're like grandmother, always reading between the lines. I did have a boyfriend, but we broke up a little while ago. That's why I left school."

"I see," Danny listened.

"I figured I'd come to Manhattan to seek my fortune."

"I think that's a wise decision. There's plenty to choose from here. "

"I want to develop my psychic gifts, and I thought I'd have a good chance of finding a teacher here, in the city."

"There are some very good ones, Cassandra, but check them out, and find the one that's right for you. Your grandmother shared Mrs. Veilo's prophecy concerning your future, and I'm certain she was correct. In all the years I consulted Mrs. Veilo, she never led me astray once. So I'm sure you'll find what you're looking for."

"That's reassuring, Danny, but what I need right now, is an apartment. Do you know of any available?"

Danny lit up like a Christmas tree.

"I certainly do. The lady down the hall from me is moving to Florida at the end of the month, and she hasn't sold her co-op yet. It is a fabulous two bedroom with a river view, and a wood burning fireplace . "

"Fabulous! Do you think I could see it?"

"No problem, I'll talk to her today, and we'll get it for you, if you like it. She's only asking $150,000. It's a steal."

Cassandra glowed inside, it seemed the fates were smiling upon her today.

"Good, now I'm ready for lunch."

The lunch at the Russian Tea Room was great as usual. They talked like the old friends they were for over an hour, until Danny had to get back to the shop for an important client. Cassandra liked the idea of being in the same building as Danny, and having a friend so close by. It felt like being with family.

Chapter 18

When Wednesday evening arrived, Cassandra took a cab from the Plaza to an old building on the corner of Ninth Street and Fifth Avenue. She immediately recognized the old Fifth Avenue Hotel as the address at which she had her first reading from Ginger Veilo many years before. She took this to be a good omen. She looked up *Mind Development* on the building's directory, then took the elevator to the second floor where the center was located.

She was greeted by a young man who welcomed her to the center, and asked her to fill out a visitor's card. He directed her to a lounge area, and asked if he could bring coffee or herb tea. Cassandra thanked him and asked for herb tea.

The people attending the seminar seemed ordinary in the positive sense of the word—secretaries, doctors, business people, and a few New York theatrical types. She felt at ease with the group, and blended with the others as they sat down to hear the Center's leader and founder, Ronald Richardson.

Richardson was a handsome man, somewhere in his mid-to-late fifties. He had twinkling blue eyes, and a shiny bald head, looking somewhat like a benevolent Mr. Clean. Cassandra recognized him immediately as the pilot in her dream. He introduced himself as Uncle Ronnie, and the audience laughed. Cassandra knew she had found her teacher, and a sense of well being swept over her.

During the two hour introductory lecture, Richardson told the audience of his life and how he arrived at being a teacher of mind-development. Before teaching the course he had traveled with a Hindu swami who had come to this country from India. Richardson was a reporter assigned to interview the swami for a television segment on eastern religions, and was so impressed by the swami's attitude and sincerity that he became a convert from his own religion of Judaism, and joined the swami as a renunciant.

Seven years later the swami died and Richardson left the order, going back into the entertainment industry. He became a talent coordinator for a television show, and booked Gregory Goldman, an aerospace engineer who worked on the NASA Space Program, for his show.

Goldman postulated, like so many others before him that there were four different types of brain waves: beta, alpha, theta, and delta. He taught a course demonstrating to students how to use the different frequencies of brain wave to relax, think creatively, and develop psychically. Richardson enrolled in the Goldman classes, and found they worked in opening the student to the powers of the mind.

After completing the course he became a certified instructor of the internationally known Goldman Seminars. However, after two years of seeing many of the Goldman graduates going back into the world emotionally unprepared to deal with their new-found gifts, he decided to open his own school. By incorporating the more balanced yoga exercises he learned from his training as a Hindu monk with the Goldman techniques, Mind Dynamics was born. The school had been in operation for nine years, and was extremely successful in achieving its goals of balanced, carefully supervised training for its students.

Immediately after the lecture, Cassandra enrolled in the course, which began classes in two weeks. During the initial six-day seminar, the students would learn to slow their minds at will and stay in the alpha state. While in alpha, they would learn to increase their energy levels, enhance learning skills, develop powers of concentration, and finally develop psychic potential. Cassandra left the lecture room that evening, knowing she was going in the right direction. Her life seemed to be changing for the better and she was enormously relieved.

Danny Darcello arranged for Cassandra to see the apartment down the hall from him the day after the Mind Dynamics Lecture.

Cassandra was in a very good mood and felt extremely lucky. She took a cab from the Plaza to a good address on New York's fashionable upper east side. She wasn't quite prepared for the cement, steel, and glass high-rise monstrosity looming before her. It felt impersonal and cold from the outside but, once inside, her feelings changed.

The enormous lobby of the building was decorated like an English castle, with a doorman dressed similarly to the English Beefeaters she had seen at the Tower of London. The walls were panelled in heavy, carved walnut, and-the floors were of imported Italian marble, covered with thick oriental rugs of the best quality.

The two-bedroom apartment was light and breezy, with an unobstructed view of the East River from every room. There was a balcony off the bedroom, designed like an Italian garden with fruit trees, statues, and a beautiful fountain. Cassandra couldn't believe how quiet the apartment was. Situated on the north side of the building and on the thirty-first floor, it was above the noise and dirt of the streets below. It was priced at only $150,000, a bargain for the size and location.

Unlike many people, who were afraid the city would collapse financially, Cassandra believed the city would eventually be bailed out of its financial straits by Washington. She was aware of several other fine psychics who had already deserted the city, believing it to be situated on a fault that would be prey to a killer earthquake of horrendous proportions, but she believed the city was safe for the next several years, and refused to worry about it.

She had to get on with her life, and the co-op seemed perfect. She would buy it, and decorate it with Danny's help. Yes, her luck had taken a turn for the better, and she was thankful.

Cassandra eagerly anticipated the six day seminar at Mind Dynamics. The initial course was given over a consecutive six day period, or, for people who were unable to complete it during one week, on three consecutive weekends. Cassandra decided to take the course six days in a row.

Danny didn't mind the breather either because Cassandra almost wore him out with their shopping jaunts furnishing her apartment. She decided to stay at the Plaza until the entire job was completed; she saw no reason to move in until the place was finished to her satisfaction.

On the first morning of the seminar, Cassandra arrived at the old Fifth Avenue

Hotel at eight-thirty. The class wasn't slated to begin until nine, so she stopped in the coffee shop for Sanka and a bran muffin. Another person she recognized from the introductory lecture was having breakfast too, so Cassandra walked over and introduced herself.

"Hello, I'm Cassandra Collins. Didn't I see you at the Mind Dynamics Seminar last week?"

"Why yes. Please Join me. My name is Megan Monroe. I've signed up for the classes. Have you?"

"Yes, I guess we'll be in the same class then. It's nice to know someone else in the class."

They hit it off immediately. Megan was a Ford model. She had modeled in all of the major magazines, both in the States and Europe, and was taking the course to find inner peace. While many of the other models were living high, and blowing their money on cocaine and good times, Megan wanted to develop her mind and save her money to buy a large farm in Virginia, her home state.

The girls were so wrapped up in their conversation that they were almost late for the beginning of the seminar.

Cassandra glanced at her Cartier watch.

"Megan, it's five to nine, we better get going."

"Gee, you're right."

They hurriedly paid the bill and left to get into the elevator.

"How did you hear of Mind Dynamics, anyway?" Cassandra asked.

"My ex-boyfriend, Jonathan Clemmons took it, and recommended it highly to me."

Cassandra recognized Clemmons' name as that of one of the biggest directors in Hollywood. He wouldn't recommend something if it wasn't the best.

"So I decided Johnny was right, and after hearing Richardson speak the other night, I was impressed."

"How did you sign up?"

Cassandra replied, "I don't know, Just intuition I guess."

"Sounds like a good enough reason to me."

The girls got off the elevator and entered the Mind Dynamics Center where they would spend the next six days.

The seminar was everything Richardson had described in the introductory lecture. During the six days,

Cassandra and the other students learned to slow their minds and go into the alpha state at will. Previous to the class Cassandra would slip into this state and have psychic flashes. However, they only happened sporadically and she felt she was never in control of her gift. The Mind Dynamics training changed all of that for her, for now she had it under conscious control.

In alpha, she could think creatively, solve problems, and tune in psychically to anyone's physical, mental, spiritual, or emotional state,by concentrating just upon their name, age and location. Cassandra developed quickly, learning to fine-tune her natural talent, much to the amazement of Megan and the other students. She began reading the other students, telling them about their families, careers, personality, dynamics and health.

Despite his outward good humor and convivial attitude Richardson was an extremely serious and dedicated teacher. All during the six day seminar he was attentive to the students' needs, and interested in their comprehension of what they were learning. Unlike many others in the "personal growth" field, he wasn't interested in turning out robot-like human products, but was concerned that each individual received exactly what would help them the most from the course. Many were there at the prodding of a well meaning friend or relative and some came on their own after reading a story in a newspaper or magazine, or seeing an interview with him on television.

Out of every seminar, there was usually one who was a seeker of truth, a seeker like himself who realized that there was more to the world than met the eye, and who wanted to understand why they were on earth and what their role might be. Cassandra was one of these fellow seekers, and Richardson immediately recognized her. The distinguishing characteristic was her already developed psychic awareness. It was almost like having young Mozart come to a teacher for music lessons. Her presence excited him because he realized he could help her achieve greatness, a greatness few in any century ever realized.

He also recognized that Cassandra was different in other ways. She was obviously well schooled and didn't have the "needy" look of many students. He could see from her manner of speaking, and her clothes, that she was used to the finest things that life had to offer. He also knew that Cassandra was aware of his gift, as a teacher.

Richardson explained to Cassandra that she must have developed this talent in other lifetimes. The idea totally captured Cassandra who, although raised as a Roman Catholic, fully believed in other lives continuing beyond the gates of death. The possibility of reincarnation made total sense to her. Richardson was totally convinced of the verity of reincarnation. He offered to regress Cassandra after the seminar was completed to find out where she developed her remarkable gifts of clairvoyance. Although Richardson made it a policy never to play favorites with students, he knew she would become his number one protege; so he undertook it to oversee every step of her development.

At the end of the six days of class, Richardson invited Cassandra into his private, book-lined office to have a talk. Cassandra was aware that this was not the routine policy of the school, and interpreted it as a sort of honor. After some initial small talk,

Richardson got down to the point.

"Cassandra, in all my years of teaching this course, I have come across a few people who have shared your psychic talents, but never once have I encountered a student as sincere and committed as you. May I ask what you are planning to do when you leave here?"

Cassandra replied hesitatingly.

"I really don't know. I came here to learn more about my gift, and how I could help people with it."

"Let me make you an offer, Cassandra; I would like to personally oversee your development. I would like you to stay here at Mind Dynamics as my assistant. You will have some administrative duties, and during the time you are here I will teach you everything I know. When you and I feel you are ready, I will help you set up a psychic counseling practice. Then you will be on your own.

Tears filled Cassandra's eyes. She realized Richardson, too, was psychic, and in this profession for the sake of helping people grow in consciousness. For the first time since Peter left her she felt a complete sense of trust and peace.

"I would be honored to work with you." Cassandra hugged the man, who for the next two years would becorne her guru, father confessor, and best friend. Their relationship began on the premise of mutual respect and admiration, and both were willing participants in the teacher-pupil relationship, proving once again the ancient adage, "when the student is ready the master appears."

Chapter Nineteen

It took about seven weeks for Cassandra to complete the purchase of the co-operative apartment from Danny's neighbor. Cassandra kept busy working at the Mind Dynamic Center six days a week, studying with Richardson in her spare time, and consulting with Danny on the decorating scheme for her new home. In the meantime she was already growing tired of living at the Plaza. She had to laugh to herself, so many people would be thrilled to spend two months living at New York's premier hotel, when after only two weeks she was ready to move on.

Danny's help with the apartment proved invaluable. He made certain the apartment was painted pale blue, according to Cassandra's wishes. All the furniture from the Designer and Decorator building had been put on rush and, as each piece arrived, Danny had it put into place immediately. All the antiques from Sarah's estate had also been moved in, and after they were situated correctly, the co-op looked magnificent.

Mrs. Maxwell, the woman who sold the apartment to Cassandra, left her the three Waterford crystal chandeliers along with mirrors in the living and dining rooms. She also left the patio garden intact and the imported hand carved Italian pink marble mantleplece. Danny insisted Cassandra finish decorating the apartment with silk and wool oriental rugs. When Cassandra moved in, the apartment looked like a French Palace, and felt like home.

Danny and his lover Donald decided to give Cassandra a huge housewarming. They compiled a guest list of over fifty people, and had the party catered by the head chef from the Waldorf. All of Sarah's old New York friends were invited, the "old guard" as Cassandra affectionately dubbed them, along with her brothers, sisters-in-law, Megan Monroe, Richardson, and other new friends from Mind Dynamics. She also reluctantly invited Elaine Martin and her roommate, Colleen.

Danny decorated the outside balcony with beautiful oriental lanterns and small Christmas lights. He hired the best disc jockey from the hottest gay bar in town for the music. He intended it to be a party Cassandra would never forget, the very first in her new home.

Cassandra felt lucky to have Danny in her life. He was right: what she needed was a party to give the apartment some "life". Cassandra was pleased that out of the fifty invited guests, she only received three cancellations, one, an old doctor friend of her grandmother's who wasn't at all well, and Elaine and her roommate.

Elaine called to tell Cassandra she was scheduled for a flight to Los Angeles and couldn't make the party, but wished they could have lunch sometime soon. Cassandra had mixed feelings about Elaine. Now that her life was going well she wasn't sure she wanted to bring back memories of Vermont to cloud her present happiness; but being softhearted, she made a date for Elaine to come to lunch the week after the housewarming. After Cassandra hung the phone up, she realized she hadn't been to see Elaine since before Christmas.

True to Danny's intuition, the party was a smashing success. Cassandra felt entirely grown up hosting a party as lady of the house. Sarah would have been proud of her. She had her hair in a chignon, and wore a white satin dress designed for her by Bobby Daniels, an important designer who had a loft in Chelsea. Cassandra went through the entire evening on a cloud, but she wished Sarah were at her side. And she wished it were she and Peter inviting people to their home, not a single woman living alone in Manhattan. She never let this undercurrent of emotion show, and managed to have a good time.

The week after the party Elaine came up to have lunch with her former college roommate. Elaine was more curious to see Cassandra's apartment and finagle a reading out of her than to visit with her. Elaine breezed into the apartment fifteen minutes late.

"Cassandra" she said, hugging her. "How good to see you."

"Elaine, you look terrific."

Elaine had a fabulous tan, was almost

anorexically thin, and had her long frosted hair pulled back into a braid. She really was attractive, Cassandra thought to herself, if only she weren't such a bitch .

"How have you been?" Cassandra asked her.

"Fine." But she really wasn't paying any attention to Cassandra, only gawking at the incredible apartment.

"Gee, your place is great."

"Thank you. I like it, it feels like home. My friend Danny did it. He is getting *Architectural Direst* to do a feature on the place next month . "

"Lucky you."

They went into the dining room where Cassandra had the table set with her grandmother's bone china and best silver. She had baked a spinach quiche and had some fresh croissants from Dumas Patisserie delivered. They chatted about things in general, and eventually got around to Cassandra's training at Mind Dynamics.

"Cassandra, I would hate to impose on you, but do you think you could read for me? I mean if you need the practice."

Cassandra complied, "Of course, I'd love to."

She really was interested in finding out

what made Elaine tick. How could a girl who was given so much by seemingly fine parents be such a spoiled brat?

The reading was disturbing for both Cassandra and Elaine. Cassandra took her deep breaths and prayed for guidance while Elaine rudely took out her nail file and began playing with her long acrylic nails. Cassandra closed her eyes and began her attunement.

She described Elaine's life as a jet-setting stewardess to a "T." It really appeared Elaine preferred her life to be totally without responsibility. She loved the excitement of different cities and different men every other night. Cassandra never realized how shallow Elaine was until she read for her and tuned into her energy. She discovered Elaine had herpes, and knowingly infected many men, not telling them of her condition. She bordered on manic depression and was becoming increasingly addicted to Valium and alcohol.

Elaine appeared to Cassandra as a young soul, who hadn't incarnated many times upon the earth, and had chosen "the school of hard knocks" to learn her many lessons. At the end of the fifteen minute reading Cassandra saw the image of a jet exploding, interpreting it to be symbolic as well as precognitive.

Cassandra told Elaine to quit her job as a stewardess, get a job more down to earth, and to go into therapy. She felt she had great talent with children and could go back to school to become a counselor for disturbed youths. Cassandra cautioned her to stay off jets for the next month, as she felt her life was in imminent danger.

Several weeks later, Cassandra received a tearful call from Elaine's mother. Cassandra had the morning off from Mind Development and was enjoying her morning coffee and croissant on the patio overlooking the East River. It was a beautiful day in May when the air was clean and fresh. Cassandra was gazing at a pigeon drinking from the bird bath on the terrace, when the phone rang. In her stomach, she felt it was bad news. She answered the phone apprehensively.

"Hello."

"Hello, Cassandra. This is Elaine's mother."

"How are you, Mrs. Martin?"

"Cassandra, did you see the morning news?" she said, sobbing.

"No, I haven't."

She knew something awful had happened to Elaine .

"Elaine was killed this morning in a plane crash."

"I'm so sorry, Mrs. Martin. Is there anything I can do for you?"

"Yes, if you would. Mr. Martin and I are too devastated to think right now. If you would go to her apartment and help her roommate sort her things out, I would be extremely grateful."

"Of course, I'll go this afternoon."

"Thank you, dear. I'll talk with you soon."

As Cassandra hung up, she ran to the front door to pick up the morning paper, which she usually didn't read until evening because of all the bad news. There it was, HIJACKED JUMBO JET EXPLODES KILLING ALL ABOARD. Elaine was one of the stewardesses on a flight to Miami Beach and the jumbo jet she was on was bombed by a Cuban terrorist. The passengers and crew were killed, fulfilling Cassandra's unheeded prophecy in horrible detail. The chills went down Cassandra's spine as she looked at the high school graduation photo of Elaine. She shook her head to herself, but didn't shed any tears, thinking to herself, what a waste of a life.

That afternoon Cassandra kept her promise to Elaine's mother, and joined Colleen in cleaning out Elaine's room and belongings. Colleen had to rush out as a substitute stewardess on a flight, so she left Cassandra with the keys and asked her to use her own judgment about what to keep and what to throw away. She directed Cassandra to Elaine's room and bid her good day.

Cassandra looked into the room; it obviously hadn't been cleaned in weeks. There were clothes strewn everywhere, and the bed was unmade. On her dresser there were bottles of every color nail enamel, and hundreds of dollars worth of cosmetics . Cassandra didn't know where to begin . She packed up her jewelry case in a big cardboard carton with some of her photo albums.

She saw Elaine's precious diary next to the night table. Not being able to resist the temptation to pick it up, she flipped through to the entries of the preceding fall at Trinity.

It is quite a revelation reading another's private thoughts about you in a journal or diary, almost like the shock of seeing yourself on a home movie or hearing your voice on a tape recorder. It is at the same time fascinating and disconcerting. Reading in the diary of a dead person is even stranger in some respects, because the person isn't alive to refute, change, or modify the perceptions recorded in black and white .

Cassandra began reading about herself. When Elaine met her, she described Cassandra as a real loser. Later, when she discovered her psychic gifts, she cultivated the friendship as useful to her. As Cassandra read on, she remembered Sarah's voice saying: "Remember, my dear, not everyone wishes you well in life." How awful to find out first hand what she meant. Why hadn't she listened to the inner voice telling her not to trust Elaine?

She vowed to keep her distance from people until she knew them better. Cassandra skipped over the entries on Elaine's personal life but she almost flipped out when she read Elaine's entries on Peter Brown. It seemed all along Elaine wanted Peter, but he never paid any attention to her. All the while, Elaine feigned friendship with Cassandra, she tried in vain to sabotage her relationship with Peter.

Cassandra began to shake inside, and had to lie down. She pushed the blanket over the bed and continued reading. Elaine couldn't understand why such a "hunk" picked Cassandra over herself. Elaine was terribly irate that Peter refused to acknowledge her presence, except as Cassandra's roommate. The entry that disturbed Cassandra the most was when Cassandra was in the hospital with the miscarriage, Peter stopped by to speak to her, but Elaine told him she wasn't in.

Why didn't she tell her? What did Peter want to say to her? Goddamn that lying bitch.

Cassandra was heartsick. She felt as if someone just stabbed her in the stomach with a knife and was turning it slowly. She got up from the bed and ran into the bathroom, vomiting all her rage into the toilet, flushing away her emotion into the bowl of swirling water.

Chapter Twenty

Finally, the day Cassandra had been awaiting arrived. Richardson felt she was grounded enough to handle experiencing her past lives. He was well versed in the technique of hypersentience, one similar to hypnosis, except the subject was, at all times, aware of the surroundings and aware of everything happening. Cassandra was an excellent subject, and her sincerity in approaching the sessions made them especially valuable as a learning experience for other Mind Dynamic students. For their benefit Cassandra permitted the sessions to be taped.

She lay down on a carpeted floor with a pillow behind her head, and a light blanket over her body. Richardson counted her down from ten to one: "and with every deep breath you take, you will go to a deeper, more relaxed, more aware state of mind . . ."

Cassandra proceeded to go into the alpha state, where she was instructed to locate her spirit guide. A beautiful man, wearing a peach-colored robe, promptly appeared to Cassandra, and identified himself as Father Galen, her inner teacher. His face appeared serene, and ageless, neither young or old. His head was bald, and an inner light and wisdom seemed to emanate from his eyes. He explained telepathically, to Cassandra that he would guide her to the askashic records, where she would be able to read the records of her past incarnations.

They proceeded to a magnificent white marble library. Galen led Cassandra up the staircase to a large room where a scribe, identified as Timothy, welcomed her, and questioned the purpose of her visit.

Cassandra replied she was seeking this knowledge in order to understand herself better in the present life, and to enable her to utilize her gifts to their fullest potential. Seeming satisfied with Cassandra's reply, Timothy granted her request and led her to the Hall of Records where Cassandra sensed the presence of other figures who did not appear clear to her.

Timothy directed Cassandra to a large stack of books where the Book of Life was located. He handed her a large golden volume, encrusted with aquamarine. A symbol of the lotus was engraved on the cover of the book, which she knew to be the symbol of spiritual unfoldment. As she opened the pages of the book, she began to see her past lives unfold.

This was confusing, so Richardson asked her to ask to see only the three lifetimes having direct bearing on her present life.

Cassandra's teacher immediately understood the request, and she was directed to the first lifetime of consequence to her present incarnation. Cassandra immediately saw herself as a small woman, with shiny black hair, and delicate hands. Cassandra had the feeling of well being, accompanied by a sense of lightness, as if she were somewhere floating on a cloud. She was aware of the lifetime she was seeing, as if she were a participant in a movie with herself being the main character As the movie suddenly slowed down, she was aware of emotions, at once experiencing them, and at the same time feeling outside of herself watching herself react in an almost schizophrenic state. Cassandra knew she was in the ancient Orient, and this woman, dressed in a beautiful pink and gold embroidered kimono was, indeed, herself. In that life, she was court harpist for the emperor. She was very much in love with an herbalist doctor who later became her husband. Tears filled Cassandra's eyes, as she recognized this wonderful man as Peter Brown from her present life.

She recalled in detail their idyllic life together, their home, and their beloved children. In the half hour spent recounting this life, Cassandra realized where she learned the value of serenity. In her present life she loved to spend hours alone at the piano, and with her painting in deep concentration. She also understood her love of the Orient and why, as a child, she insisted upon wearing Sarah's Oriental bed jacket around the house.

The instant attraction to Peter was also clarified; why she fell in love with him at first sight was clear. Her heart began to ache at the though of the loss of Peter when Richardson directed her to turn the pages of the book to see her next important lifetime.

Cassandra found herself in the body of a male, about age forty, living in Judea at the time of Christ. Her name at that time was Lucius, a bachelor, and a professional soldier in Caesar's occupation army in the Mideast. For some time, Lucius heard rumors about a spiritual teacher named Jesus, who had traveled the area for several years, doing magic tricks of one sort or another, and talking of the spirit life, here and hereafter.

Lucius, being a pragmatist who liked the good life of earth, dismissed the talk as some hysterical babblings of the mystical Jews, whom he did not understand nor care to know. He preferred his life in the army, with its decent wage, good wine, and willing maidens to sample his physical charms.

Lucius was called by Pilot to be one of the men whose duty it was to crucify the man called Jesus. Although the teacher claimed he wanted no earthly power, Pilot wanted him dead, since he believed he incited many Jews to revolt. As a political enemy of the State, he was to be put to death by crucifixion. It was Lucius' job to see his commanding officer's wishes carried out.

On the day set for the crucifixion, Lucius saw the golden haired man being beaten unmercifully by the other men, tormented and spat upon. Jesus took this punishment without a word. As he was crowned with a wreath of thorns, Lucius looked into the man's deep blue eyes and was shaken. Never before had he seen or witnessed such peace emoting from another being.

He ordered the men to stop this mistreatment of the prisoner, and they reluctantly stopped. Lucius went to his commanding officer and personally refused to crucify a man who was obviously not a criminal of any sort.

Because of his actions, Lucius was court martialed and sentenced to death himself. In that lifetime, Cassandra learned the value of courage which began a turning point in her spiritual evolution from flesh to spirit.

The final incarnation Cassandra was privileged to see was the lifetime immediately preceding her current one. She appeared as a lovely Spanish girl, Rosario, who was orphaned at birth. She was raised in a convent by an order of teaching sisters, who were wealthy, being supported by the King. She was happy at the convent and was groomed to become a nun herself. She recognized the Mother

Abbess, who showed her special favoritism as Sarah.

When the Mother Abbess died, Rosario no longer desired to be a nun. It seemed she met a very handsome gypsy man who repaired many broken things around the convent. Unbeknownst to Rosario, he was married. They fell in love, and she became his mistress. She ran away from the convent to live with the gypsies.

When she went to the gypsy camp, she learned her lover was already married. All the women scorned her, except for the man's mother, a clairvoyant. She lived with his mother, and became her student, developing clairvoyant gifts, learning to read Tarot cards and palms. In this lifetime, Cassandra recognized the old gypsy woman teacher as Richardson, who was once again teaching her to use her "second sight"

Before she left the altered state Richardson asked her what her main purpose for incarnating in this life. Cassandra realized she was meant to develop perfect balance in this lifetime; balance between her personal life and her work, between her body and mind, and between her intellect and emotions. She would work as a clairvoyant counselor, a kind of "psychic Joyce Brothers", popularizing spiritual teaching through the media.

As Cassandra rushed through what seemed to be a time tunnel of sorts, she opened up her eyes, feeling completely exhilarated. She wasn't aware of being "out" for more than two hours. It seemed minutes at most.

An inner peace settled over her; things formerly puzzling made total sense. Richardson cautioned it would take several days to integrate the experience into her present life. Cassandra remembered her grandmother's favorite saying, "all things in due time."

Yes, she thought to herself, all things in due time. Any sense of urgency which formerly possessed her, melted away as she realized how many lifetimes it took to get to this point. She had a new understanding of the Oriental mind with its sense of patience and waiting.

All things in due time.

Chapter Twenty One

Because Richardson had seen too many talented "children" go into the world with unripened psychic gifts wreaking havoc on their own lives and the lives of those who came to them for guidance, he warned Cassandra of the dangers of the psychic path. He cautioned her to be balanced and grounded so her life would work.

He encouraged her love of ballet and theater, and her painting. He explained that because of operating in alpha for longer periods of time than most humans every experienced she had to guard against mental imbalance. She must combine physical activity and outside pursuits so she wouldn't go off the deep end mentally like so many fine and well intentioned psychics before her.

Richardson knew Cassandra's desire for enhancing her gift was serving others through counseling. The people who entered the field for ego aggrandizement and financial gain, failed to attain success in the field or happiness with the gift. This was the reason Richardson himself didn't set himself up as a psychic reader. He didn't want the enormous hassle in his life that he had seen others go through. He would rather teach and coach others, staying in the background where he felt he could accomplish the most good.

Cassandra was given biographies of the great psychics who went before her to study. She learned she was not alone in sharing this talent. Edgar Cayce, Eileen Garrett, and Arthur Ford were some of the best who had lived in the twentieth century. With Richardson's training and her own abilities, Cassandra intended to join their ranks.

Richardson also saw that Cassandra read books on counseling, psychology, yoga, reincarnation, and philosophy. He started her off reading *Winged Pharoah* by Joan Grant, the story of Grant's previous incarnation as an Egyptian Pharoah and psychic. Cassandra studied *Autobiography of a Yogi* by Yogananda, to understand the mind of a genuine yogi master and Indian philosophy. She read books by Gina Cerminara, Jess Stearn, and Thomas Sugrue, about the life of Edgar Cayce, the "Sleeping Prophet" of Virginia Beach.

In the two years Cassandra remained at the Mind Dynamics Center she received an incredible education. When Richardson could teach her no more, he sent her on her way with a polished skill, and a deep understanding and appreciation of her gift to become the premier psychic of New York. Richardson's unselfish fatherly interest in Cassandra paid dividends for the school as well, for after her graduation, she became a Patron of the school, seeing that it never had any financial lack. She considered it her Alma Mater, her church, her home; it filled the void Sarah's death left.

Megan Monroe began sending all her model friends and photographers for readings. Megan would come in every three months or so for an update, not wanting to let any career or personal opportunity slip by. She had never before encountered anyone as psychic as Cassandra, or as dead-on accurate. One of Megan's closest friends was Timothy Lavelle, photographer for many newspapers and magazines as a papparazzi.

Late one afternoon, when Megan was in his studio he asked her, "How about going out for a drink, Megan? I'm beat.

Last night I was covering that bitch Kelly Trachard; I was running all around town trying to get a few good shots for People. These rock stars are totally insane and with the hours they keep, I'm up all goddam night long."

"Darling, I'd love to another time. I have an appointment in a half hour with my psychic, and I wouldn't dare be late."

"You go to a psychic?" he said surprised. "You don't seem the type. I mean, you're so normal."

"Listen Timothy, this lady I go to, Cassandra Collins, is also a friend. I met her at Mind Dynamics two years ago. All my good business deals she advised me on, and remember that loser, Anthony Dahl? Well, she told me three months before his arrest as a coke dealer to get rid of him he was bad news. Cassandra is incredible, you should go see her sometime." Megan handed him one of Cassandra's cards.

"Yeah, maybe I will. See you later."

Megan exited his large loft in Soho; he sat down at his glass-topped bar, and poured himself a vodka on the rocks. He had never been to a psychic before, he didn't even know if they were for real. Having been raised as an Italian, he was wary of the evil eye and some things his mother taught him were better left alone and he believed psychics to be one of them.

Unfortunately, he didn't ignore his gargantuan sexual appetites, which got him into lots of hot water over the years. He had three children by two different wives, whom he had divorced and he was paying exorbitant alimony and child support. Now he had to work hard to pay for his past sins. He didn't think a psychic could tell him much. The only thing puzzling him was whether his missing sister would ever be found, and why she suddenly disappeared from her Westchester estate. He decided, "what the hell. I'll call this bimbo, and see if she's any good."

He called and made an appointment. Cassandra was booked weeks in advance. After only two years as a professional psychic she had no cancellations. Richardson was right, if you are for real in New York, the world is your oyster.

A month later, Timothy showed up on time for his appointment. As Cassandra began reading for him she sensed his skepticism, and wryly commented on it.

"Timothy, it is very curious as to why you're here, since you really don't believe in psychics at all. However, you are concerned about your sister and her welfare." His pupils dilated as Cassandra hit him directly with his one question. She asked him, "Do you have a picture of your sister with you?" He happened to have one in his wallet.

"Yes, I do." He took it out, hands sweating, swallowed, then smiled, "you're terrific."

Cassandra focused on the photograph of a lovely Italian girl. The name Teresa came to her.

"Is her name Teresa?"

"Yes, it is."

Cassandra closed her eyes; she saw a hill covered with leaves and some boys playing hide-and-go-seek by a railroad track. She then saw a black plastic garbage bag with a hand protruding from it. She then saw a man in a London Fog raincoat leaving the scene and she opened her eyes.

"Timothy, when did your sister disappear from home?"

"About six months ago."

"I feel she has made her transition. She

was murdered. Her body will be found by two boys in the fall, somewhere near her home by railroad tracks?"

Timothy was shaken to his soul. Never before had he experienced anything like he was feeling now.

"I never believed she would run away, and not tell the family."

He started crying and Cassandra held his hand.

"It must be very hard for you; is there any way I can help?"

"Yes, if there is any way you can find the bastard who did this horrible thing, and help us to locate the body."

Reluctantly Cassandra agreed. Several times in the past she had volunteered to help the police in these matters, but the vibes in those cases were usually horrendous, especially in cases of child abduction, where there was often sexual abuse followed by kidnapping and murder.

Cassandra closed her eyes and once again focused on the picture. She saw the house where Teresa lived with her husband, and she saw Teresa thrilled when she discovered she was pregnant. Her husband, Victor, came home and upon discovering her job of being pregnant, got drunk and beat her unmercifully. Teresa fell, hitting her head against the fireplace. She died almost immediately. He panicked, then stuffed her body in the back of his Cadillac, and buried her in a makeshift grave by the railroad tracks in the middle of the night.

After the reading, Timothy went to a detective in Westchester with the story. Cassandra sketched out a map of where she thought the body would be found. When the police got to the location described on the maps two boys were playing hide-and-go-seek nearby. When the police came upon the spot Cassandra had described they found the decomposing body of Teresa just as the reading stated.

Cassandra didn't want any publicity from the case and, true to his word, Timothy kept the whole story out of the papers, but he told all of his clients, and relatives, who deluged Cassandra with requests for readings. Her waiting list went from one week to six weeks and she stayed very busy. She loved reading for the clients, helping them with their problems, and helping to direct their lives in positive channels for good.

But privately Cassandra was lonely.

All the success in the world didn't compensate for the emptiness she felt in her personal life. If it weren't for her friends she didn't know how she would survive. Everyday she thanked God for Danny, Richardson, and Megan. They loved her, and cared for her, but she longed for the feelings she had when she was with Peter in Vermont. She wondered if she would ever know such complete happiness again?

Chapter Twenty Two

As the July fourth weekend approached, Cassandra received a call from her brothers. They built a large beach house in South Hampton for the summers, and called to invite her for the long holiday weekend. In the two years Cassandra worked for Richardson at Mind Dynamics she never allowed herself to get romantically close to any man, preferring to get over her broken heart.

Cassandra seemed to have taken on a monastic existence of sorts, doing her readings, teaching a few psychic development classes, painting her lovely watercolors, which she bestowed on family and friends on holidays, dinners with Danny and Donald, lunches with Megan, and weekends at Mind Dynamics with Richardson and the other students. In two years, she hadn't traveled off the Island of Manhattan, except to attend dinners on Long Island with her brothers on the holidays.

First, Tom called her to persuade her, and when he was unsuccessful, an hour later Ryan called. It seemed they would not take no for an answer. Their wives and children were in Europe on a tour so they promised that there would be total peace and quiet at the house. Cassandra gave in and decided to go. The Mind Dynamics school was closed for the weekend, Megan was off doing a shoot in England, and Danny and Donald were on Fire Island for a two week summer vacation.

Cassandra decided it would be better to spend the weekend with her brothers than to spend the time alone in her ivory tower. Cassandra's needs as a woman had not been met in the two years since Peter Brown disappeared from her life. Cassandra was afraid she would never be able to love anyone else with the same intensity she felt for Peter. She had been asked out on numerous dates over the past months, clients and students at the school were crazy over her, but Cassandra felt the time was not right. However, she was in a very sexy mood and decided she was going to make the weekend count.

She ran over to Bergdorfs and bought a skimpy emerald green bikini that set off her auburn hair to perfection, and made her blue eyes appear aquamarine. She bought an oversized beach hat and bottles of Bain de Soleil sunscreen to protect her fair Irish complexion from the sun's ravages. She went to B. Dalton's and bought a big romantic novel to read on the beach. She intended to let herself go and simply have a good time, something she had almost forgotten to do with the seriousness she had been demonstrating lately.

Tom and Ryan enjoyed Cassandra's company, they found her sense of humor a delight, but they cautioned her from the start of the holiday that they didn't want her lecturing on metaphysics, or Mind Dynamics. Also, they asked her not to criticize their choice of girlfriends either. Since their wives were vacationing in Europe, they didn't see any reason not to sample some of the sweet girls of the Hamptons, and they didn't want Cassandra pointing out reasons. Cassandra promised to keep mum on all accounts. Little did she realize, it would be her brothers who would be critical of her that weekend.

Cassandra left the beach house early to take a quiet walk on the beach. She put her feet in the water, decided to take a swim, and washed away accumulated layers of stress in the soothing tide. She stayed in the water about an hour, frolicking in the waves and body surfing. From the time she was a small child, she had an affinity for the ocean. She and her brothers were good swimmers and learned to ride the waves into the shore. Time passed unnoticed by Cassandra.

From the shore, a handsome gray haired gentleman in his early forties sat down staring at the beautiful red haired mermaid he seemed to have discovered. Cassandra blushed when she realized he was looking at her, she wondered if the waves had knocked part of her swim suit off, or something. As Cassandra walked out of the water and ran up to where she had left her hat, sunglasses, and towel, the gentleman walked over to her, and said very nonchalantly, "Miss, do you have the time? I seem to have lost all tract of the hour simply mesmerized by you in the surf ."

"The time for what?" Cassandra shot back. She always seemed to have a remark after someone had left, this time it was on the tip of her tongue, and she let him have it.

"Very good, indeed. Allow me to introduce myself, Philip Kingston." He politely bowed his head.

Cassandra couldn't help smiling, "Cassandra Collins." He took her hand and she felt the electricity he generated. His eyes were as green as the summer ocean, and his body didn't have an ounce of fat.

"May I sit down." he said, already sitting next to her.

"Be my guest," she smiled.

Cassandra always admired strong men who knew how to get what they wanted. Philip was one of these men. In less than an hour she knew his educational background, Ivy League all the way, Princeton undergraduate, Harvard Law: his hobbies, tennis and golf, and his address in New York.

The only thing puzzling Cassandra was the lack of a Mrs. Philip Kingston. Men that good looking and forty were either married, divorced, gay or lying, and from the looks of Mr. Kingston, he was married and cheating. Cassandra closed her eyes and psychically saw an attractive blond woman with three boys.

She cleverly asked, "And oh, by the way how are Mrs. Kingston and your three boys?" Philip almost choked.

"I wasn't aware you knew my family, Miss Collins." His sudden switch from Cassandra to Miss Collins tipped Cassandra off that she touched a nerve.

"I don't know, Mr. Kingston. Just psychic."

"Psychic? Yes, how fascinating, I have always been interested in parapsychology. Do you do readings?"

"Yes, I do."

"I'd love to have a reading from you."

"Sounds like a line to me."

"It is."

"I'm flattered." Cassandra smiled.

"How about dinner tonight at eight."

"I'd love to."

"Aren't you afraid of having dinner alone with a strange married man?"

"No, should I be?" she asked coyly.

He paused, "Where shall I meet you?"

Cassandra pointed over her shoulder, "The house over there, you can pick me up after you meet my brothers."

"It's a date. See you at eight."

Philip got up and sauntered down to the beach. As he left Cassandra realized she was glad she decided to leave Manhattan for the weekend. Yes, she was very glad, indeed.

Philip Kingston wore a white linen suit with an open blue silk shirt. He looked great, and he knew it. Cassandra came to the door and greeted him in an off-white sundress. She had her long hair pulled back with a blue ribbon, and wore no makeup. She looked ravishing. Both were arrned with the knowledge of their power for an evening of games. Cassandra's psychic gift gave her an additional advantage, one she intended to use later in the evening. After all, he was safe wasn't he? He'd never leave his proper wife, and Cassandra was in need of some tender loving care.

Philip invited her over for a candlelight dinner at his beach house. He had white roses on the glass dining table, and a chilled bottle of Beaujolais waiting. Brie and grapes, the standard fare at the Hamptons that season, were ready and waiting, and Cassandra was faintly amused. He had set everything up for the seduction, and he wasn't aware that he was the one about to be seduced.

Philip had some Ferrante and Teicher background music on the stereo system, not realizing the music gave away his age, but Cassandra thought it to be a nice touch. She bet he would be a good lover too and if he wasn't, it wouldn't be Mother Nature's fault, for that morning on the beach she had glimpsed an outline of considerable endowment, and she intended to see whether it met her expectations.

Cassandra was pleased with herself. She had her diaphragm in her pocketbook, along with spermicidal foam. She was determined there would be no accidents this time, unlike with Peter, there was no illusion of love or romance. For more than two years she had lived as a nun. But her brothers would have said, "none in the morning and none at night."

Tonight she would relinquish her role as a psychic and become a woman, a state she remembered once brought her a great deal of pleasure and heartache. Cassandra was no glutton for punishment, and she intended to stay as uninvolved as she could with Philip. This would certainly be a challenge .

The dinner was fabulous; Philip was a gourmet cook. They had filet of sole Florentine, caught fresh that day, chocolate mousse for dessert, which he admitted he bought from the Chi-Chi Dessert Shop, and a delightful spinach salad with mushrooms and bacon on top.

Cassandra let Philip play out his hand. She was saving hers for later. The only thing bothering her throughout the dinner was wishing she were here with Peter, not Philip. After dinner they retired to the big deck that looked out on the moonlit ocean. A few children had set off fireworks, and some of the houses set off Roman candles and different pyrotechnics of amazing color.

It was a warm evening. Cassandra sat on the white wicker couch, and Philip sat next to her. He poured a brandy for himself and asked if she would like some. She deferred, saying she thought she had enough already. At that moment Philip gave up hoping she would be sharing his bed. Then Cassandra played her hand. She very lightly brushed his crotch on the way to picking up her purse to get her Dunhill's. As Philip grasped her hand and lit her cigarette, Cassandra wondered if he got that neat maneuver from watching Cary Grant in *North By Northwest*? Well, wherever he got it, it worked. He was suave and she was interested.

She threw her head back and inhaled on the cigarette, and as she did, he kissed her neck sending a bolt of electricity to her toes. She was certain he would be a good lover. As he nuzzled her neck, she put out the cigarette. He nibbled her ear whispering, "Cassandra, you are the most desirable creature I have ever beheld." True or not, she didn't care. She wanted to believe him, and to experience life again.

She gave herself to him. He removed the spaghetti straps from her dress and, as it fell exposing her beautifully rounded breasts, he caressed them as if she were a goddess. His touch was certain but gentle, and he kissed her on the mouth with a joy and sensitivity that brought out passion she had repressed for two years.

Cassandra responded in kind, and he gently removed her dress, and began covering her perspiring body with kisses.

She felt like a puppet, obeying every subtle command of his powerful being. They made love in an orchestrated dance like two incomparably matched dancers, complementing each other perfectly. Cassandra fantasized he was Peter as she experienced pleasurable wave after pleasurable wave. Her body weak and exhausted, she dissolved into Philip's arms, feeling a coldness steal over her heart as she realized Peter, her real love, was somewhere else, and she began to weep.

Philip was inside thrusting, and mistook her tears for Peter as tears of joy, he screamed as he came inside her. He sexually desired this woman whose soul he could never possess, and whose mind he would never understand.

They returned to the bedroom and immediately fell asleep, Cassandra dreamed of Philip's socialite wife and three children. She felt something was wrong with his marriage and she vowed to clarify this issue before venturing any further into his life. She was already ensconced in his libido; she didn't feel she warranted or wanted a place in his heart.

Cassandra didn't want to hurt anyone, let alone Philip. Although on the outside he was confident of his every move, she realized that inside he was a romantic little boy who would be devastated if he ever learned of her indifference.

Cassandra vowed never to let on about her feelings for Peter, and swore that he would never find out what was going on inside her head. Although they would be physically intimate time and time again, he would never share her secret world.

Cassandra erected a barrier around her heart protecting anyone from entering and hurting her. As she rationalized in her own mind, she became guiltless as a little child walking naked on a beach.

Chapter Twenty Three

In the morning, she awoke to see him lying beside her, and as she felt him stir, Cassandra pretended to be asleep. From the corner of her eye, she watched him rise from the bed, his morning erection huge, making his way to the bathroom. He was like a beautiful animal. His bronzed nautilused body, and graceful movements reminded her of a jungle cat. He was an exquisite lover and Cassandra was grateful.

When he climbed back into bed he rolled her over and kissed her softly, at the same time entering her from the rear. At once the drowsiness left her as if she was being swept away blindly on the wings of passion. He kissed her neck and shoulders as his fingers gently played with her clitoris. He was filling every void in her mind with passion and she loved every second of it.

Philip was a man experienced in the art of love and she was a willing student. She went into rapture, as they simultaneously climaxed. Philip held her close, and once again drifted off to sleep, smiling and contented, their senses satisfied, leaving only their souls hungering for more.

Later in the morning after brunch with Philip, Cassandra walked down the beach to her brothers' home. Philip had to see a client and she wanted to take a bath and do some reading. As they parted, Cassandra promised to see him later for a drink. The twins were in the living room reading the morning papers, as she entered, slightly disheveled from the evening's tryst.

"Guess we know who got lucky last night, Ryan," Tom said smiling. He was happy to know Cassandra had been out, enjoying herself .

"Sure enough, brother," Ryan replied with a smirk. He didn't believe in equal rights for women, and unlike Tom was a total chauvinist.

"Who was he, Cassandra?" Tom asked sincerely.

"Oh, you met him last night, Philip Kingston," she replied.

"Hope he likes Irish stew." Ryan laughed uproariously.

"Glad you find it so amusing, Ryan. It is nice to have a man appreciate one's more subtle virtues."

"Oh, is that what they're calling it these days, Sis?" Ryan was belligerent.

"What is your problem, Ryan?" Didn't you get any last night?" As soon as the words slipped out, she regretted speaking them.

Ryan was livid, "I'd like to slap your little slut face. Don't talk to me that way."

"Hey, calm down you two," Tom intervened. "We're not twelve year odds."

Ryan cooled off a bit. "I guess you're right."

Cassandra was hurt by her brother's remarks. "What I do is my business, and what you do is yours. From where I sit, what is fine for the goose, is fine for the gander."

"Cliches just keep popping out of your mouth," Ryan mocked her.

"And they will keep popping out as long as you see fit to criticize me."

Cassandra stormed out of the room, and fled to the privacy of the bathroom. She took a long soak in the tub, reflecting on last night's revels with Philip. She wasn't sure what she was doing was moral, but for now, she was content to wash last night's sins away.

All day long Cassandra glowed, feeling alive once again. She had almost forgotten herself as a woman the past two years and Philip Kingston had helped her revive. Although she was pleased to realize life was good in all its aspects she was concerned about Philip's marital status. She decided to meditate about the situation and decide what she should do.

She closed her eyes on the big deck in front of the beach house, and made herself comfortable in the shade.

She concentrated on Philip and his family. The first person she saw was his wife. The name Gloria came to her mind. She saw her as a tall, regal looking woman in her early forties with long black hair, standing in front of a two story brick house in the suburbs of New York, which she felt to be Westchester.

It flashed on Cassandra's inner eye that the address Philip had given her was one where he stayed during the week alone. He must live with his wife and children on the weekends. She had the picture firmly in her mind, and she vowed to confront him with this information before venturing further with him. Then she would decide whether or not to continue seeing him, but for the moment she felt lucky to have such a good lover in her life.

Cassandra avoided her brothers all day. She didn't like Ryan's attitude toward her. After all, she could take care of herself; being an orphan didn't mean she was helpless, far from it. But she didn't want any more confrontations this weekend, and she was looking forward to seeing Phil later that evening. She went out on the beach with her novel and relaxed for the first time in what seemed to be eternity.

Phil stopped by after a game of tennis with another lawyer friend from the city. He was sunburned and sweaty, but to Cassandra's eyes he looked gorgeous. He grabbed her to give her a kiss, and as he kissed her she melted. Realizing her brothers might barge in any minute, she pushed him away.

"What would you like to drink?"

"You, on the rocks."

"You'd better tell me, otherwise you'll get nothing."

"I wouldn't bet my life on it."

Cassandra noticed he was sporting an erection underneath his tight tennis shorts. She figured she would put him in his place. She went over to him and patted him on the head like a puppy.

"Good boy, go down. Play later." Phil was at once furious with her, and highly amused. He began laughing, "You're too much Cassandra. I'll come back later."

As he got up to leave, Cassandra gave him a passionate kiss. As he left, he realized she was desirable and a tease to boot. That was fine, he loved games, too.

Later in the evening, Cassandra walked over to Phil's beach house. The air was alive with the smell of the sea and gunpowder. Children had been out all day shooting off fireworks. It reminded her of the fireworks in bed the previous night. She was content though she didn't know whether she would ever see Phil again after this beach weekend. She didn't care.

She was learning so much about herself she didn't much concern herself with the future. But the past still haunted her. Why did she pretend it was Peter she was in bed with? She knew she hadn't let him go. She might have been two years without a man physically, but she held Peter to her with all her might. She knew if she ever wanted a healthy relationship with a man, she would have to release him. But she didn't want to.

Cassandra believed, like a true romantic, he would someday share her bed and her life and she was not ready to give up that hope or dream. With these thoughts in mind Cassandra commenced the relationship with Philip Kingston, who had thoughts of his own.

Philip hadn't slept with his wife since the birth of their youngest son, seven years earlier. She refused sex with him and said if he insisted on sexual union, she would divorce him and she would poison his sons against him. He would lose everything. She would make up rumors of how he beat her and raped her, and other fantastic lies.

Gloria was mad, totally out of her mind. She was beautiful, rich, socially aware, but demented. She burned their first home down after she decided she didn't like the color scheme. When he listened to the psychiatric report he couldn't believe he had unknowingly married a schizophrenic. She would go weeks, perhaps months, perfectly fine, as if everything was grand. Then a little incident would set her off. She only exhibited this behavior to those closest to her, because in the community she enjoyed a reputation as a gifted harpist, member of the Chamber Orchestra of New Rochelle, and she was a social leader of the Episcopal Church.

She had been raped when she was

only eight years old by her lesbian camp counselor, but her parents refused to believe her. This resulted in her always pretending everything was fine on the outside when, in reality, it wasn't. After the birth of their third child Philip realized something was amiss when she refused to have sex with him and threatened him with all the wild lies. Philip was afraid of her and, in order to keep peace, took an apartment in New York, and came home only on weekends.

Philip loved his three sons more than anything else ln the world, and would never divorce her until the children were grown and on their own. Right now the youngest was seven years old so Phil resigned himself to the fate of living a separate life from Gloria. lt presented no problem because he had never become lnvolved with another woman. He preferred his sex with high-priced call girls until meeting Cassandra.

Chapter Twenty Four

After hearing Philip's story of his unhappy marriage Cassandra didn't feel guilty for sleeping with him. She knew the story he was telling was the truth; she could always psych into lies. She knew she would only like Philip, and he would fall in love with her. She wasn't certain of the reasons, but she did know they would respond differently.

She was a romantic and dreamer. He was a realist and plotter. Though the sexual chemistry was there she would never be able to bare her soul to him as she had to Peter. He was a business man, a pragmatic, salt-of-the earth type, a sexual athlete. Out of her loneliness, she accepted what was being offered. So Philip Kingston entered Cassandra's life and her bed in New York. Because she wasn't in love with him, she insisted he keep his own apartment. Every morning, he would go home, check his answering machine, and depart with his myth intact of the married man with his own apartment, remaining in the city on business.

Philip was a shrewd businessman and well-known lawyer. He was also influential in the Democratic Party. After they had dated for several weeks, he suggested to Cassandra that she hire his publicist/agent, Sally Springsteen to catapult Cassandra to fame.

Philip was correct. After the introduction, Cassandra was certain of Philip's good judgment. Dealing with the media was Sally's business, and the woman was something else. Sally had nerve and a cunning sense of timing.

To be a talent agent one had either to be born rich and do it as a hobby, or be born hungry and desire to get to the top at any cost. Sally had been born the latter. Without the advantages of money, looks, or breeding, she developed chutzpah. Sally fought and clawed her way to the top, using every meager weapon in her arsenal.

Raised in the area of New York City known as Hell's Kitchen, Sally soon learned you needed street smarts to survive. Her parents, Solomon and Selma Springsteen, were simple Russian immigrants who eked out a meager living barely feeding their brood of seven undernourished children. Sally's parents had heard America was a land of plenty, and before the Revolution managed to arrange passage to America. Finding support from fellow Russian Jewish immigrants, they fell into the blight that was the life of poor people everywhere, never escaping from the mentality that created the ghetto. The went from one hell hole in Minsk to the other, Hell's Kitchen in Manhattan.

Sally vowed she was moving up and out, armed with secretarial training in New York Public Schools, and a High School Diploma from Harren High School, she found a job in the William Morris Agency as a secretary. She worked and slept her way to the top. Her father used an old Russian proverb, "If you had to fuck to get a job, you had to fuck to keep it." Sally never minded working or fornicating and figured she was lucky to have both. She never thought about the finer implications of her actions.

She became an agent, and by God she. intended to be the biggest, if not the best. After ten years, several thousand dollars saved, capped teeth, and a botched nose Job, Sally bought her own IBM Selectric typewriter, rented office space and installed a phone. She was in business. After stealing stationery from the Morris Agency and three clients, she was on her way to the top. Like many successful people she never bothered to look back.

Sally booked Cassandra's first radio appearance on a morning radio show, WMPA's Harris Harrold's Show. Harris was a thirty-eight year old English stud with a wicked sense of humor and uncontrollable libido. The minute he saw Cassandra, he wanted into her pants. Not believing in the powers of the mind, beyond "who", "what", "where", "when", and "how", and how many times he could get it up, he gleefully bated Cassandra with questions, as the home listeners were able to call in and ask their questions.

Cassandra tried to relax by taking three deep breaths, at the same time remembering her agent's advice to remain bright, up, and positive. "Remember darling, they want Doris Day not Sigmund Freud at 10 o'clock in the morning." Cassandra asked each caller for birthdate, month, year, and time of day, as she rapidly looked up each in her Ephemeris, as she used astrology as a psychic tune-in for each one. After twenty minutes elapsed and seven people had drained her psychic energy, Harris was amazed. His conscious mind remained skeptical, so he caustically asked, "How come you never say that so and so, who calls in, is a low life of the worst sort, a murderer, thief, or whoremonger? Surely not everyone is as you paint them, now are they?"

Cassandra realized Harris was a total buffoon. He should have gotten down on his knees that very minute to thank the powers that be, which enabled his meager talent to rate a showcase, listened to by two million people daily.

Instead of honestly telling him how she felt, she replied, "Harris, the job of any psychic or astrologer worth his salt is to find the spark of divinity in a person and then fan it into a flame."

Harris replied, "Very good, very good. Did you hear that ladies and gentlemen? Find the spark of divinity and fan it into flame. Very well, now we must thank Cassandra Collins for visiting us on the Harris Harrold Show. Cassandra you must come back again soon."

"Thank you, Harris" Cassandra replied, relieved to be dismissed.

While the commercial for a clothing store in New Jersey was played, Harris shook Cassandra's hand, and out of curiosity, made an appointment to see her privately.

During the following two days, through the radio station, Cassandra received 346 pieces of mail addressed to Cassandra. Her career as a media celebrity was launched. She became a regular guest on Harris' show, and was offered her own spot on Sunday nights after a sex therapist. Cassandra accepted on the advice of Sally, who stood to make a fortune on Cassandra's gift and pleasing personality.

Soon Cassandra and Sally were flooded with requests for local appearances. The first she accepted was the local Breakfast Show, hosted by two former Los Angeles talk show hosts, Bryan Bantam and Serena Eggleston. Bryan was a fiftyish former song and dance man who made good as the sidekick of a successful evening talk show host. He decided to branch out on his own, and did very well in the 1960's and 70's with the proliferation of celebrity talk shows. When the next decade rolled around and cable television began decimating network television, Bryan was relegated to a "put-out-to pasture" position of hosting a local show. Serena was a contrast to her cohort. Beautiful, young, ex-model, university trained, she was up-to-date. *Interview* magazine recently did a feature interview on her.

Cassandra was picked up by a cab and sped over to the television studio on Columbus Avenue and 67thth Street. She was ushered into makeup and hair and scheduled to be featured on the third segment. In the Green Room she was offered a bagel and coffee, which she graciously declined. A page asked her to sign a release form, which the network used. She wished Sally had come with her this morning, but when asked, she replied, "Now darling, you don't need me there to hold your hand, do you?" The show went well, as usual.

Cassandra made up her mind to fire Sally when she had time to find a good agent. This was not the time. Like a general once said, "Don't change horses in mid stream," or some other such words of wisdom. Damn it.

Sally was a shrewd publicist. One day during lunch Cassandra recounted a dream about Prince Charles and Princess Diana. In her dream she had been watching television when it was interrupted by a news bulletin. The scene immediately turned to Prince Charles and his entourage, which included Princess Margaret and Princess Diana leaving the family home in Sandringham. All of a sudden the camera flashed to the roof, where behind a large chimney, an IRA soldier in a ski mask was shooting with a rifle. The camera focused on the crown price slumping over, a bullet in the chest.

Cassandra was shaken by the dream, and through her friends in the BBC got in touch with Scotland Yard. Sally listened as if she weren't impressed, but after the luncheon she slipped away and called her friend Naomi at the Focus, a weekly tabloid with an incredible circulation. The following day Cassandra's picture was on the front page with Sally's version of the dream. The headline blared "Psyhic's Bloody Vision of The Royal Family Rocks Britain." Inside there were pictures of the castle, a description of what Cassandra saw, and an embellished version of the Scotland Yard story.

Cassandra couldn't believe Sally

would violate a private trust so blatantly. Later, when almost every major talk show called to book her, she realized that Sally's killer instincts, however base, were right on the mark. Cassandra was just too exhausted to fire Sally, so she kept the greedy bitch, and kept following her suggestions. Cassandra didn't want to make her life any more difficult than it already was. In her gut she knew that Sally was a cut above the devil, but as an agent she knew her business. Maybe that was why she was known in the business a "La Cunt." As Philip so cogently stated, "The contrast to her makes your art look even better, so don't fret." Cassandra knew he was right.

Chapter Twenty Five

Cassandra was besieged with people with all sorts of problems and dilemmas from broken marriages to lost dogs, catastrophic illnesses, and curiosity seekers. Rich and poor, young and old, they found a way to her door, and all were welcome. Desiring to protect the anonymity of her clients, and detesting answering services,

Cassandra had an answering machine installed which led to giving her the nickname "Genie". Whenever the phone rang on the public line, (she had her private number just for her closest friends), the machine would pick up with soothing harp tape in the background, saying, "this is the Genie of the answering machine, my master is unable to speak to you at the present time, at the sound of the tone leave your name and telephone number. Your call will be returned as soon as possible."

Cassandra employed a student from the Mind Dynamics School as secretary to return calls and set up readings, and screening the nuts who wanted to harass psychics. Cassandra had astrology charts run off on a computer, using the chart as a tune-in to her subconscious mind for a reading.

Her reputation earned a great deal of money which she had no need for but she realized, like the therapists always say, "If they pay, then listen, learn and get better." Cassandra charged, realizing even without her inheritance, she could have supported herself very well in New York. She had a feeling of inner satisfaction. She was not only successful at what she loved doing, but was supporting herself at it to boot!

Philip was a lesson in endurance for Cassandra. Always in the back of her mind she realized their relationship had no future. Philip was a realist; he saw things exactly as they were and he judged future trends very well. Unlike Cassandra, he wasn't psychic, but he could logically project the present into the future with uncanny accuracy. Many times he would ask Cassandra her feelings about certain financial information or a political situation, and their conclusions would be identical even though hers came through intuition and his through logic.

Philip started life in a middle class family in New Jersey. He went to the public schools, working as a newspaper boy, and later as a caddie. In his heart, he knew he belonged in the exclusive club of the well-to-do, and he vowed someday he would belong. It was ironic that later, when he did finally belong to the best country club in Westchester County, he refused to play golf, hating if from the days he was a caddie.

The hurt little boy who felt he didn't belong surfaced. Though people may rise above their backgrounds, often they never forget the hurts and the knocks they received along the way. When it came time to go to college, he got an athletic scholarship to Brown in Rhode Island, where he allied himself with the monied classes. He studied harder than any other jock at the school, and wound up marrying his wealthy roommate's sister, from a prominent Newport, Rhode Island family.

Philip never stopped to consider whether he loved Gloria. She was from old money and he was buying his future financially and politically, and he intended to play the part well.

As a youngster, Philip wasn't sexually active; he sublimated his sexual energy into making money and athletics, always concerned about securing his future. His only sexual experience prior to marriage was masturbating in front of a mirror while he flexed his well-muscled body. He spent hours in the gym perfecting his form; watching himself in the mirror gave him a thrill no woman ever managed to surpass.

Philip was an athletic lover. Cassandra could never complain about him physically, but she was always left with the feeling he was a sex machine lacking heart and soul. When Cassandra mentioned to Philip on one occasion that she thought he could use a therapist to discuss his problems, he brusquely turned the remark aside, commenting, " If it works, don't fix it."

During the last seven years of his marriage to Gloria Philip's only sex had been with prostitutes. He paid plenty and was assured of discretion from Manhattan's best call girl service. Because he paid top dollar, he was used to getting his pleasure wherever and however it took his fancy. Cassandra had a great deal of adjusting too in that area, for although she was deeply passionate, her only experience in the bedroom was with Peter. Cassandra knew Philip stopped seeing other women.

Sometimes he was so incredibly demanding he almost wore her out. Cassandra felt in some ways inadequate when it came to sex, because she hadn't had any experience in fellatio and was unable to admit her lack of experience to Philip. Philip explained to Cassandra he loved being sucked, a habit he got into with the ladies of the night, and one he was unwilling to break.

One morning several weeks after her first tryst with Philip, Danny Darcello knocked on Cassandra's door for a morning chat and a cup of Cappuchino. Cassandra was always glad to welcome Danny, but this morning he realized she was somewhat upset.

"What's the matter, Princess? Something wrong with your new boyfriend?"

"Oh, he's fine, Danny. I think there's something wrong with me."

"Anything I can do to help, just ask. You know I'm always willing to help you out, Cassandra."

Cassandra smiled at him; he was so kind, he was the best friend anyone could ever have, and then she thought, "Why yes, there is something you could do for me." A blush began to creep over her fair Irish neck and face.

"Why Cassandra, you're blushing. What is it?" Danny's curiosity was aroused.

"Danny, I'm at a loss for words, I really don't know how to say it?"

"Just spit it out."

Cassandra started laughing, "If you only knew how funny your remark is. Danny, Philip loves fellatio more than anything, and although I've read two marriage manuals, I'm afraid. Would you help me?"

Danny began laughing, "Of course, my dear, in my days I've had plenty of experience. Everyone must learn sometime. Get me a banana and I'll show you."

Cassandra watched transfixed as Danny proceeded to give the banana head that would put any monkey to shame.

Later on that evening, when Philip and Cassandra were in bed, Cassandra went to work on Philip with her new knowledge. Philip was very pleased. After making love, Cassandra asked Philip, "Well, big boy, how did I do?"

Philip laid back on the pillow satisfied and leered, "For a beginner, I'll grade you an A minus."

"Is that all? I thought I did rather well."

"Practice makes perfect." He laughed and began another round with Cassandra.

True to Philip's nature, in the following weeks Cassandra received plenty of practice. Within a month he had graded her A plus, and gifted her with a beautiful Cartier diamond necklace for doing such a good job on her report card.

Philip lived life to the fullest, and Cassandra loved accompanying him on his business trips. He showed her a great time, taking her to the finest restaurants, best hotels, and all the latest shows. He was a break from her intense days as a psychic counselor. With Philip all she had to be was beautiful and fun. Cassandra accepted the relationship for what it was worth. She knew it would never lead to the altar, and she didn't mind. It was fine for right now.

Philip also helped her career at every turn. She was convinced he was the married gypsy from her past life, and was, in this lifetime, repaying the karma he owed her. Whether or not it was true, the rationalization enabled her to continue the relationship.

Philip was a true Anglophile. When he was called on to go to London for three weeks on a specialized case he asked Cassandra to go with him. She was delighted to go. It had been years since she had been to London with her grandmother, and it would be wonderful to revisit the spots they had seen together, now with the eyes of an adult. She wanted to visit Stonehenge where the Druids once lived, and other magical spots on the islands. When Cassandra and Sarah went on the Queen Mary it had taken many days to cross; going on the Concorde, it took only a few hours.

Philip loved going first class – if it was expensive, he lusted after it, whatever it was, from his Porsche to Cassandra. Cassandra never discussed her finances with Philip, but let him know she was well off. She never took a penny from him, but was old fashioned enough to let him pay for everything. Cassandra had a set of standards and she adhered to them.

Philip bought her a little throw pillow for Valentine's Day from Harrods, embroidered "Good Girls Go to Heaven, Bad Girls Go Everywhere." She smiled when she unwrapped it, but in her heart she knew she too was going to heaven, because she fundamentally believed herself to be good despite the norms of society. She was true to herself. After all, he was only the second man she had ever been to bed with in her life so she wasn't exactly promiscuous.

Philip loved theater, so every night in London they went to see a different play, opera, or ballet. Cassandra, too, adored drama and music so they made a good couple. If only she could love him, but it seemed love was reserved for Peter. Philip was a good lover and Cassandra, if not totally happy with her lot in life, wasn't complaining. She let Philip sleep late and work out at a gym in the day while she went about the town sightseeing. She loved the city's people, the friendliness she saw in all the bright faces; it was unlike New York with its aura of despair.

Cassandra felt at home in England and, if circumstances had been different, would not have minded living there. But their weeks together convinced her she was better off living alone.

Chapter Twenty Six

Philip indulged Cassandra's fancies. He wanted to make certain she was happy in her role as his mistress. Although Cassandra was convinced the only person Philip would be able to entirely love was himself, she believed he loved her as much as he could ever love any woman. Philip was undoubtedly the most self-centered man she had ever encountered. Because he viewed the women in his life as a reflection of his character, he treated them well.

If they didn't respond in kind, he banished them from his world.

He was a true narcissist. He was obsessed with his appearance, and spent more time in the bathroom getting ready than Cassandra. This never bothered her in New York, because every morning after he spent the night, he would return to his own apartment to get ready for the day. On vacation it tried her patience.

Philip was concerned about every gray hair, every ounce he managed to put on an because he loved wine and good food, he disciplined himself to work out at a gym every day. Someday he expected to hold public office, and the public always votes for the best looking candidate. He loved to cite the Kennedy-Nixon television debates as a case in point. He had already had his eyes "done," collagen injections in his smile lines, and hair plugs where he was beginning to thin.

Cassandra wisely kept her comments to herself because she knew if she offended him he would become sulky and take out his anger in bed. Cassandra was romantic and didn't like anything rough, but she was aware of his predilection for perversion. She never wanted to push

Philip to the edge where his anger was not under control. He never neglected his regimen so Cassandra managed to spend time alone every day sightseeing, meditating, reading, or shopping.

Being a well known theatrical lawyer, Philip was invited to all of the major theatrical events and premiers on Broadway's Great White Way. He was invited to an abundance of dinners, parties, and soirees and he proudly escorted Cassandra, as if she reflected his success. Everyone knew Cassandra was his mistress, and they didn't much care.

Cassandra was such a pleasant companion, and Gloria such a bitch, he would prefer being in Cassandra's company any day. It was chic to have your mistress blatantly accompany you wherever you went during the week. On the weekends, Philip was in attendance at the large Episcopal Church in Scarsdale with his wife and children, but during the week he did what he damn well pleased. In the entertainment world different and even aberrant lifestyles were tolerated. Creative people didn't bother with the conventions of suburban people.

Cassandra and Philip were invited to the movie premiere of *Justinian*, a multimillion dollar porno picture. It starred several well respected movie stars, and fabulous sets, interspersed with sleaze. Cassandra had her doubts about going, but Philip insisted. Cassandra had never seen a porno picture and Philip thought it was about time. After all, even Jackie O. was photographed in line waiting to see *"I Am Curious Yellow."*

The premiere was covered by all the major networks and publications. The papparazzi were out in full force. As Cassandra and Philip pulled up to the movie theater in the limousine, Philip directed the driver to pull around the corner. He hated being photographed, and didn't want anyone to record his presence at the premiere with Cassandra. They managed to enter through a side door unnoticed.

The pornographer king producer of the movie and his girlfriend, who owned *High Rise* magazine were buying their way into New York society and were very successful. The parties at their townhouse in midtown Manhattan rivaled the best given by Hugh Hefner at his Playboy Mansion.

Philip loved the movie, but Cassandra

was extremely uncomfortable. She had known that some of the practices go on, but seeing them in 70mm in the presence of strangers offended her. My God, what would Sarah think of her granddaughter now? After the movie the producer invited Philip and Cassandra to the premiere party. The townhouse, where the party was held, was a combination of two adjoining townhouses with an interior fitting royalty — marble steps, an enormous entrance hall, complete with a television monitor system.

Downstairs was a Roman style swimming pool. There were priceless paintings everywhere. Cassandra thought to herself "Pornography must be a very big business." She psychically flashed that Philip was the lawyer for this snake and his corporation. So that was where Philip made his money. He never mentioned his clients.

Philip had political aspirations and would never divorce his wife; he preferred to keep up the facade of marriage. He avoided being photographed with Cassandra. Philip was very self protective, and Cassandra realized he would run for office and win. His past, however spotted, would never harm him because, like a good Indian scout, he always covered his tracks.

Cassandra saw Philip as having the instincts of the deprived child; he would never be happy until he attained his goal of supreme worldly success. She hoped he didn't fail to realize it when he finally attained it. Philip filled a void in her life, but she realized she would never have a satisfying emotional relationship until she released him. She hung onto his physical presence, as she hung onto Peter's emotional presence with scorpionlike tenacity. Holding onto the dream, even if she stung herself to death.

Chapter Twenty Seven

Cassandra's career was blossoming beautifully. *People* magazine sent a reporter and a photographer to do a three page feature on her, and she made the cover of the magazine. She was featured in a dynamic *Playboy* interview, a first for the magazine to interview a psychic. She was offered a cable talk show on the Lifetime

Network, which was to start broadcasting in several months, and NBC was syndicating her Sunday night talk show nationally. Cassandra was becoming a bonafide media celebrity. The media was touting her as the Richard Simmons of the psychic world. Her advice to people was accurate, compassionate, and quick. Everyone was happy with the way things were turning out, except Philip.

The more successful Cassandra became, the less demonstrative he became toward her.

The once fabulous lover was now becoming a selfish bore in bed. One evening after a really fine radio show, Philip showed up in his limousine to pick Cassandra up at the NBC building in Rockefeller Center. At midnight on Sunday evenings in downtown New York, the streets are deserted, except for an occasional street cleaner or security guard. Philip struck up a conversation with the guard at the door of the building. He recognized Philip from his picture on Page Six of the *Post*, and realized he was the same man who usually accompanied Cassandra to her radio appearances on Sundays, when he was on duty.

"Good evening." Philip said nonchalantly.

"How do you do, sir? Nice evening we're having."

Philip noticed the small radio on the small table near the door. "Did you happen to hear Cassandra Collins on the radio tonight?"

"Yes, I did. I never miss her program, even when I'm at home. She is some fine psychic. Yes, she is."

Philip smiled, but at the same time was annoyed. Now that he and Sally helped build her career, she was more famous than he. Whenever they went out to dinner or to friend's homes, she was the one everyone wanted to talk to first.

He felt his role was becoming that of a personal escort and he didn't like it. He knew it wasn't Cassandra's fault – it was just that everyone seemed to want to know about themselves, and she was just so damn obliging. Well, he was the star in their relationship and he would prove it to her tonight. He had been drinking heavily which didn't help his reasoning.

Several minutes later, Cassandra breezed out of the doorway all aglow from the rush of a show well done. "Hello, darling." She kissed Philip on the cheek.

"Hello, Charles." She smiling broadly at the doorman.

"You were real fine tonight, Miss Collins."

"Thank you, Charles." She waved goodnight as Philip opened the door to the limousine. Philip was obviously agitated, and Cassandra didn't know why.

"Darling, I am exhausted. Let's go home." Cassandra said breathlessly.

" All right with me. I thought you might want to go for a ride down to Battery Park or something."

"Another time, Philip. I am beat. It's after midnight, and I have a client coming at ten."

"Suit yourself." Philip said. Cassandra could hear the coldness in his voice and smell the whiskey on his breath.

"Is something wrong, Phil? " She was really concerned . She knew he hadn't been right for the last few weeks and she was wondering about the reason.

"No, everything is fine, just fine." He replied sarcastically. In his mind, he felt like telling her to get out of the car and walk home. The lovely little girl he fell in love with on the beach existed in his mind no longer. Only a successful, poised young woman remained with the world at her feet, the world he believed he had put there.

"Philip, we have got to talk, you have been so moody these last weeks. Have I done something wrong?" Tears filled her eyes.

"Yeah, just about everything."

Cassandra was devastated. She tried so hard to make their life together good, and he seemed to try to thwart her at every turn.

"What is it now."

"Cassandra, let's face it. You don't have time for me anymore."

"What do you mean?" The hurt almost kept the words from coming out.

"When we met, you were young and vulnerable. Now you're just a hardened bitch. Just like the rest of the whores who used me."

Her hurt turned to anger. "I am sorry you feel that way, Philip, but how can you call me a bitch, when I have been so good to you?" She was crying and shocked.

"Just forget it." he said, turning away from her. The car pulled up to Cassandra's building and the driver got out and opened the door. Philip got out first without waiting for Cassandra and walked to the door quickly. Cassandra followed, mystified by his behavior. He was showing a side of himself she had never glimpsed before.

The night doorman was savvy enough not to say anything as they entered the building. They walked hurriedly to the elevator. Once inside the elevator, Cassandra looked at Philip with tears streaming down her face, "Why are you acting like this? I don't understand."

They walked in silence down the hall to her apartment. As soon as they were inside the door, Philip grabbed Cassandra and shook her. "All I have been to you is an escort, a meal ticket. Well now I'm going to get my money's worth."

Philip threw her down to the floor and began to rip her dress off. Cassandra screamed, "Stop this madness, Philip. You're acting like an animal." Looking into his eyes, she was frightened. For the first time in her life she felt fear for her life.

Throwing his body across her, Philip pinned her down and forced her mouth open with his tongue. Cassandra bit down as hard as she could, and felt the warm, salty taste of his blood spurt into her mouth. He pulled back with a start. Realizing that she bit him, he smacked her broadly across the face. She pulled her knee with all her might into his groin. Philip cried out, rolling over in pain.

Cassandra got to her knees and made her way to the bedroom. As she locked herself behind the thick walnut door, she heard the foyer door slam as Philip stalked off into the night. Shaking and soaking wet with perspiration, she fell onto the bed and sobbed hysterically into the pillow. The man she once trusted was now a stranger.

Chapter Twenty Eight

Later in the week, Cassandra received a dozen red roses and an urgent phone call to meet Philip for dinner at *Louise Jrs.* which was one of their favorite restaurants. Although Cassandra wanted to forget what had happened, she would never trust Philip again, and wanted him out of her life for good. She agreed to see him one last time.

Over dinner Philip tried to be his old charming self, but Cassandra was wary. After some chit-chat Philip took her hands and said, "Cassandra, I've got something very important to tell you."

"What is it, Philip?"

"I'm going to seek the senate seat being vacated this fall."

"Congratulations, I knew that for months, and you know you'll win for sure."

"Cassandra, this means we can't see each other any more."

"Why, Philip?" Cassandra wanted to see him lie his way out of this one.

"Americans can stand anything from their movie stars, but their politicians have to be model citizens. With the Moral Majority in force, I can't afford to mess up my reputation. It could mean the election." Cassandra sipped her white wine, not saying anything.

"Look at me, Cassandra, we've got to stop seeing each other. It cost Teddy Kennedy the presidency fooling around, and it won't happen to me."

"Of course not, darling, take me home."

Inside Cassandra felt nothing. She shed no tears. She knew she was using Philip as a placebo for the great chasm caused by Peter's absence.

As they left the restaurant, Cassandra realized she would never see Philip again. As he escorted her to his waiting limousine he motioned for her to enter.

"Don't bother, Philip, I'll take a cab.

It wouldn't be good for your image to see you stopping in front of the apartment now, would it?"

He stood amazed, as she flagged down a cab. As she entered the yellow checker cab, she waved her hand, and he saw the diamond Cartier bracelet he gave her sparkle on her wrist. She left his life forever.

When Cassandra got home she took out her journal and began writing. She realized another chapter in her life was closing. He had been in her life almost nine years. She couldn't beieve how fast the years had flown.

She walked over to the golden Florentine cellaret and brought out a bottle of aged Courvoisier brandy. She took one of the beautiful carved Lalique brandy snifters with the smiling cherubs Philip had given her for her birthday the year before. She slowly sipped the brandy, and let the amber liquid burn her insides as she took out all of the mementos together.

One by one, she threw each one into the fire before her. When the last souvenir was burned hours later, she had put quite a dent in the bottle of brandy.

Cassandra took off the diamond necklace and bracelet Philip had given her, and put them away in a jewel box. Tossing the crystal goblet into the fireplace, she exorcised Philip from her psyche.

Deep inside she had always know he would only be an affair, and now she was glad to have him out of her life. But she was scared. She was "single" again in Manhattan, and once again must make her life alone.

BOOK THREE

Chapter Twenty Nine

The lights at the Blue Lovebird Disco were swirling as Cassandra entered the huge factory-like structure on Manhattan's West Side. The guards let her inside the press door, recognizing her by the button she wore with Bobby Daniels picture on it.

Bobby Daniels was the flamboyant English designer of women's clothing whose charity fashion show was being held that evening at midnight. Bobby, a stunning looking a man in his early fifties with bright blue eyes and curly blond hair, had been a client of Cassandra's for several years. He had been an Olympic gold medalist ice skater in the early sixties. Bobby moved to New York with his lover, a rich movie star who set him up in a dress design business. In the twenty or so years he had been in New York, Bobby garnered a reputation as the premier designer of women's evening wear; he also designed costumes for Broadway shows and Hollywood movies.

Although Bobby was gay, he truly loved women and made them look and feel wonderful wearing his magical clothes. Cassandra was no exception. From the time of her first New York party, her house-warming, nine years before, she had used Bobby as her sole designer. They quickly became very close friends. On weekends when she needed a date for a public outing, Bobby, when not involved with one or another of his "tricks", would gladly escort Cassandra. He was just what she needed: bright, good looking, poised, witty, and fun to be with, in any situation.

Whenever he needed a good looking woman to bring to social functions, she was available, leaving him free to cruise the room for available mates.

Bobby had hired the press agent of one of his movie star clients who was big in both name and size. Both the press agent and the client were two of the biggest lushes in show business and both were quite mad. The star was too drunk to appear that evening so she sent her adopted daughter as a stand-in. The girl was not half as attractive as her celebrated mother, but done up in Bobby's clothes she looked like an angel. The power-hungry press agent ran the entire show as both commentator and dictator. The show was magic, but the agent succeeded in driving away the press with her heavy handed attitude.

True to Cassandra's intuition, the agent and Bobby were in court two weeks after the show. Cassandra had seen the trouble between the two psychically, but many creative people, Bobby included found out too late how accurate and uncanny Cassandra was. Not following her advice proved to be expensive and sometimes tragic.

Another girl in the show, Melinda Day, was warned to leave the city before Christmas. She got a big job as the secretary to a local talk show host on a midday show. She ignored Cassandra's prophecy and was murdered by her boyfriend after a drug party on Christmas Eve. Although Cassandra was well loved, many people were afraid to know the truth, and avoided her counsel.

Ted Tibbetts, Bobby's current boyfriend, numbered among them. Ted was a top Broadway choreographer/director. Although many times, he would ask secondhand for word on current projects through Bobby, he would never come in person for a reading. Cassandra didn't see their relationship lasting, as she felt he would become infatuated with a leading lady from one of his plays. When the disastrous short-term affair ended, he would desire to return to Bobby, who would already be involved with someone younger.

As Cassandra climbed the stairs to the dressing room, she saw a handful of Broadway stars gathering at the impromptu bar Bobby's press agent had arranged outside the dressing room. The upstairs of the disco was crowded, but somehow Bobby and his assistants had managed to orchestrate the madness into some semblance of order, organizing the show that was to begin in less than an hour.

Cassandra went up to one of the young apprentices from the Fashion Institute of Technology and was handed her gown for the show. It was a lovely red Chinese silk kimono which accented her fair Irish complexion. Cassandra hurriedly dressed and was ushered into a bathroom for hair and makeup. A hairdresser from one of the Broadway shows pulled her hair into a chignon and held it in place with one of Bobby's sequined combs with spangles floating down from it. She dusted Cassandra's face with white powder and accented her lips with a bright red lip gloss. Cassandra looked and felt like a glamourous madam of Shanghai, a Chinese opium eater. She play acted with a "devil may care" attitude and lined up with the other celebrities for her first experience in modeling.

Cassandra was excited, she knew this night would be unlike any other she had experienced. Dressed in this exciting gown she felt her psyche transformed by the loudly blaring music; its deafening beat adding to the feeling of being in another world, quite a contrast to the soft harp music she played at home. Cassandra walked out onto the runway; she was introduced by Concetta Ellis, a black jazz and blues singer, "Ladies and gentlemen, Cassandra Collins, New York's Premier Psychic."

The applause and flash bulbs popping brought out an aspect of her personality Cassandra had never known existed before. She walked onto the runway with her head held high, and sauntered as if she had done this all her life. All the while inside she was thinking, "Grandmother, if you're looking down at your little girl, I hope you're proud." There was no doubt in anyone's mind: Cassandra had arrived.

In the audience, Bobby Daniels saw Cassandra as he never had seen her before. From the eyes of friendship, she always seemed a sort of surrogate little sister, but seeing her radiate on the runway, her beauty struck him for the first time. After the show, he made his way to the dressing area, and complimented Cassandra on the way she looked and handled herself.

"You were sensational tonight, kid." He kissed her on the cheek. "Thanks, Bobby. The show went great, don't you think?"

"Yes, and you were the hit."

"Flattery will get you everywhere," she joked.

"Why don't you come over for lunch tomorrow, if you're not working? I'd love to talk with you."

Cassandra was pleased Bobby had singled her out from all the stars for this attention. The other models shed their gowns and dressed in their street clothes and some looked enviously at Cassandra.

"I'd love to."

"Come down to the loft at one."

Bobby turned and was immediately deluged by the press and media people. Cassandra felt herself lucky to have Bobby as a friend.

The next morning Cassandra roused herself out of a deep sleep and rushed over to the Health and Racquet Club for a swim and steam to clear her head. She was not used to the late hours of the show, preferring to be in bed at a reasonable hour. She was extremely disciplined; a psychic must, like a dancer, keep the body and mind totally clear to do their work effectively. This never was a problem for Cassandra, because by her very nature she was a moderate person. She drank champagne on occasion, and was semi-vegetarian by instinct, having rare roast beef only during her period, for iron. Her single vice was smoking, although she limited herself to a half pack of Dunhills a day; she smoked in the evening after her last reading of the day had gone.

After her swim she relaxed in the sauna of the Club and meditated. She was amused by a picture she saw of Bobby in the nude and quickly dismissed it from her mind as a harmless fantasy. Why would she see him nude? After all, they were only friends. She left the sauna and went to the locker room to dress, and rushed downtown to meet Bobby for lunch.

Bobby lived in a restored brownstone in the Chelsea section of New York. His place was like a magnificent stage set for a Tennessee Williams play. It had large 14-foot ceilings, was painted black and Chinese red, and was furnished with huge old antiques that made you feel like you were stepping back in time to an era of charm and grace. Cassandra loved visiting Bobby. She felt as if she were in a world where she truly belonged. In Bobby's office was an antique brass bed masterpiece where he entertained guests, and also ran his business. The groundfloor of the townhouse held his work area. It was not unusual for Helen De Vito, his secretary, to come in early to discover last night's trick still in bed, wound around Bobby's exquisite sleeping form. Helen was a gifted designer in her own right but she chose to work for this man and devote her life to him.She loved Bobby too. It was not the typical man woman love, but love by any name is still love.

Once anyone, man or woman, was in Bobby's presence they were drawn into his aura by his incredible warmth. When the matrons from Long Island, New Rochelle, Beverly Hills, or Dallas, entered into Bobby's loft, they found what their husbands and lives outside could never give them, glamour, beauty, and understanding. Bobby was more than a designer, he was a magician.

Women bought his clothes, not only because they were beautiful, but because they transformed them into creatures of a world where problems did not exist, where women become goddesses to be worshipped, and men were interested only in winning their favors. Of course they realized it was only make believe, but it enabled them to steal moments of magic in a world where the computer was king, and beautiful women were tossed over for the financial concerns of a materialistic world gone mad.

Bobby understood exactly who he was and what his place was in these moments lives. He played his role to the hilt. The walls of his townhouse were covered with portraits of the glamour girls of the thirties and forties, and Cassandra with her classic looks fit in place among the best of them.

As Cassandra entered Bobby's loft Helen DeVito greeted her at the door.

"Bobby will be with you in a minute, Cassandra. Have a seat." She ushered Cassandra into a huge oak framed divan in the studio covered in a plush velvet fabric.

"Can I get you some coffee?"

"Thank you, Helen, that would be wonderful."

A minute later, Bobby appeared with

Larry Bailey, the editor of a magazine for the arts, which was really a front magazine for closet queens who loved to look at the cute little boys in dance outfits who graced the pages of the glossy monthly publication. Bobby's creations were a standard feature in almost every issue of the magazine, and he was friendly with everyone on the staff. As Bobby and Larry came into the room Bobby introduced Cassandra to him.

"Larry, I've got someone you must meet, my good friend, Cassandra Collins."

"Nice to meet you Cassandra, Larry smiled. He was in his thirties with short black hair and a trimmed beard and moustache.

Cassandra smiled back. "Good to meet you."

"Larry, Cassandra is the best psychic and astrologer I've every known. You must have a reading from her, and it wouldn't hurt if you had her write a column for your magazine each month."

"That's a good idea." Larry handed Cassandra one of his cards. "Call me and we'll get together to discuss the idea."

"Thank you, I'd like that."

"I'll talk to you later, Bobby. Nice meeting you, Cassandra."

"Good-bye."

Helen showed Larry to the door. After he was gone Cassandra said to Bobby, "I wasn't aware I was in need of another press agent?" Cassandra joked.

"You're right. That dragon Sally does very well by you. What you need is a good lay.

"Bobby!" Cassandra said blushing.

"You do, you know." Bobby grinned.

"Thank you very much, Mr. Daniels, but I'm afraid I haven't found any takers lately." Cassandra feared Bobby's perceptions were right on.

"Let me see if I can remedy the matter?"

"How do you propose doing that?"

Bobby quickly seized Cassandra and planted a wet kiss on her lips. She was stunned. "Bobby, I never knew you cared." She said half serious, half joking.

Bobby looked at her cautiously. "You know, Cassandra, I'm not straight. I mean after all the readings I've had with you, you ought to be the first to realize that fact. But I have always been attracted to you, and last night, at the show, I was mesmerized by your incandescence."

"Bobby, I don't know what to say." Cassandra was genuinely moved.

"Cassandra, I'd like to date you, as a man and a woman, not as brother and sister. You wouldn't be the first woman I've had between the sheets, either."

Cassandra was at once confused, flattered, and amused. Bobby was incredibly gorgeous but she had never thought of him in a physical way before. But the idea had its merits.

"Let's have lunch, Bobby. I'm hungry."

"Hungry for what?" He toyed with his words.

"Food, silly. We can discuss your Interesting proposition over lunch at length."

"At length? Hmmm, Cassandra. You really are interested."

"I guess I am", she said, a little surprised, "but don't twist my words."

Bobby smiled, "We'll see."

Before they left for lunch, Bobby left Cassandra alone on the couch, and went back into the office to leave instructions for Helen.

As he walked through the loft, he smelled the lingering fragrance of her perfume Chanel No. 5, on him.

"Helen, Cassandra and I are going out for lunch. If there are any important calls tell them I'll be back in two hours."

"O. K. Bobby, I'll tell them." Helen noticed the twinkle in Bobby's eye.

"What are you so happy about? Did we make a sale to Saks for a half million or something?"

"Nothing that mundane, Helen."

"You look like the cat that swallowed the canary."

"From your mouth to God's ears."

Helen shook her head as Bobby turned and left. She sauntered back to the workroom, muttering something to herself about life in the big bad apple making one crazy. Then she decided to go out and risk her life on the street to grab a sandwich at lunch hour, wondering why her boss was so happy.

Chapter Thirty

Bobby had planned the dinner to delight all of Cassandra's senses. He made certain nothing would go wrong. He had the entire house lit with white candles, and had four overflowing flower arrangements of white and lavender orchids on the glass top dining table. He used his best lalique champagne glasses for the chilled vintage Dom Perignon and had Belgium caviar for hors d' oeuvres. For dinner he prepared his own specialty, pasta primavera with chicken, and for dessert,the piece d'resistance, grand mariner chocolate mousse.

The rest he left to chance. He glanced at the Rolex watch his former lover, the director/choreographer had given him, and was aware Cassandra was by now fifteen minutes late. He sat down sipping his vodka and tonic; he awaited the vision of his fantasy to appear, and rubbed his crotch in anticipation of the wonderful evening in store.

As Cassandra stepped out of the limo, the driver nodded appreciatively as she told him not to wait. She walked up the stairs to the door and rang the bell; she looked stunning. Her hair was perfect and the facial she had that day at Valmy's made her flawless skin glow even more. Cassandra was dressed in one of Bobby's white evening gowns as a symbolic act to bring them closer together.

"Cassandra, you look lovely," Bobby said as he removed her mink.

"And my, what good taste in clothes."

"Thank you, Bobby. I thought somehow you might like it."

Cassandra smiled. It was hard to tell if the dress was created for Cassandra or Cassandra was created for the dress. Bobby escorted Cassandra to the oversize couch and removed the bottle of chilled Dom Perignon from the Tiffany icebucket. Popping the cork he toasted her "to Cassandra Collins, a goddess kissed by the gods."

Cassandra was stunned. Twice before men had toasted her with this saying, her father at her birth, and Peter in Vermont, and her life changed. Now she was hearing it for a third time. Bobby noticed the strange expression in her eyes.

"Are you all right?"

"Better and better" she smiled, covering her surprise. The dinner was wonderful and Bobby was the perfect dinner companion. They talked throughout the dinner, laughing and joking.

When it came time for the awkward moment of leaving or staying, Bobby said, Cassandra, I know this may be a little strange for you, but I want you to know it is for me too. I haven't been to bed with a woman in over eight years, but you're special to me. I love you as a friend, and I wouldn't do anything in the world to screw up our friendship. I want you to know that, so whatever you decide is okay with me."

Cassandra knew the truth when she heard it, and she knew Bobby was talking from his heart. She put her arms around his neck and kissed him. He led her to the big bed, and undressed her. He had never seen her naked before; her body was perfection. He kissed her gently; he undid the coverlet exposing satin sheets. Cassandra was delighted in a childlike way; this was a totally new experience, like spending a night away from home at a schoolgirl chums house, a real sleep-over party, but with a difference; Bobby was no schoolgirl.

One of the best things about Cassandra's relationship with Bobby was that he really understood her gift for tuning into people and their problems, and he didn't resent the time she spent with them. Cassandra loved the people who came to her. That love combined with her gift was the real reason for her success as a psychic. Many times she just listened to the people who came to her for help and let them lay down their burdens. Just by talking to her they felt better. If Cassandra felt they were headed in the wrong direction she would warn them and tell them to rethink their priorities.

Bobby's love for Cassandra grew every day, but he never lost his appetite for men; Cassandra, in her wisdom, never questioned him about his conspicuous absences as well as obvious infidelities. She left well enough alone. When he broached the subject of marriage she would sidestep the issue, citing their needs for privacy and separate space. Bobby felt Cassandra's love. In most ways their relationship went smoothly for them, although to many people didn't make sense.

Some days, when she was daydreaming, Cassandra imagined what it would be like to be married and have a real home, but the only face she could ever see was Peter's; the only child she would want to have was Peter's. With Phil, it had never been an issue, and well, with Bobby being bisexual, she thought it wise never to have a child with him. Besides, she knew she and Bobby would never marry. Bobby didn't really want to get married; he didn't want to have to give up his boyfriends on the side or make excuses for his behavior.

What he did want was a child of his own, an heir, a namesake, someone to belong to who wouldn't go out of fashion like a gown, or evaporate like a perfume. Someone who loved him without consciousness of style, name, or prestige. He knew Cassandra loved him for himself. She could have cared less if he was a designer or not. In her, he found an acceptance he believed he would never find in a woman, save his own mother, but Cassandra would never agree to bear his child, of that he was certain. If he did sire a child by another woman, he knew it would end his relationship with Cassandra.

Other men she did not view as threats, for she figured "boys will be boys", but another woman would threaten her femaleness, her beauty, her power, and she would not entertain the idea, let alone the possibility. Bobby knew exactly where she stood so the relationship progressed, sans marriage and sans child, but it worked, and the love between them grew daily.

Cassandra and Boby were invited to attend an intimate party for a few friends of Jimmy Jankos, the publicity director for a new fragrance firm relocating to New York from Paris. Cassandra had been introduced to Jimmy at a big soiree at a Soho loft owned by the photographer who did the head shots for her publicity pictures.

Jimmy was fascinated by psychics from the days when he lived in San Francisco. He immediately tried to monopolize Cassandra's whole evening, after being introduced to her by the photographer hostess. Cassandra was adept at being cordial, but she suggested he come in for a reading. He promptly called her the following day, and Cassandra squeezed him in, after one of her model clients was too coked-out to make it.

Jimmy arrived at Cassandra's place, wearing an Armani three piece suit.

"Hello, Jimmy." Cassandra greeted him with her biggest smile. She knew he was going to be very important in her career. The panoramic view of the East River from her living room impressed him. Cassandra sat down in her antique blue silk moiree chair in front of her mirrored French Chinoise desk. On it was a flawless Italian crystal ball which was several hundred years old, a Steuben glass starburst sculpture, and her Tarot Cards in a green onyx and brass box.

Cassandra asked Jimmy his birth date, and closed her eyes. She took a deep breath and said a prayer.

"Father, Mother God, we again seek thy presence. I ask to be used as a channel of light, and love and attunement for thy son, James Jankos. I ask that a blessing be bestowed on James, myself, and the reading in the light, Amen."

Cassandra began to see pictures forming in her mind's eye. She saw a vase of dead flowers on a table.

"You had a relationship that has died, and

you're still hanging on to it." Then she saw a handsome man in a beret.

"It is with a Frenchman." She proceeded to describe the man down to the most intimate details. Jimmy was aware that Cassandra possessed a great gift. She told him about his loves, his money, his health, and in the hour they spent together Jimmy felt Cassandra knew him better than anyone on earth.

Many times people immediately wanted to become her friend because of her psychic rapport. Cassandra was cautious about forming relationships because of her gift. She was drained by so many people that she was aware of the motives, but she sensed a childlike purity about Jimmy, and she liked him, so she accepted his invitations to dinners and lunches, and gave him advice from time to time. Although the arrangement started as a client to counselor they soon became friends. Jimmy, being a perfect Libra, introduced Cassandra to half of New York society, at least the half he knew.

Cassandra was introduced into the world of cosmetics, from the fake counts and countesses, to the tired old stars who are trying to trade in their name for a quick buck in some cosmetic or perfume hawked from shopping mall to shopping mall across star-struck land of middle America. Jimmy specified Bobby as the designer in his perfume ads.

At a dinner party, Jimmy introduced Cassandra to Mabel Fleaman, a grand old dame who ran a publicity concern pushing fragrances and cosmetics. There were Jimmy's usuals: a beautiful black opera diva from the Met, her constant companion, a bright pianist/composer, an old time hat designer for Garbo and Davis, and an artist who was sweet, but a hopeless drunk with his usual boy "soon to be star" in tow, whom he was keeping until someone better became his new diversion. Cassandra was seated next to Mabel and kept staring at the woman's nose. She asked, "Do you make your living from your sense of smell?"

The woman almost dropped, "Yes, I make my living in the perfume industry."

Mabel Fleaman got where she was because she could size up people in an instant. She recognized Cassandra's "star quality" and immediately saw her as the key to her springtime frangrance promotion. When she asked Cassandra who her agent was and Cassandra mentioned Sally Springsteen, a look of ice came over her eyes. "I'll get in touch with her."

Inside the woman thought, "My God, I hope this girl knows what she's doing mixed up with Sally. She's the biggest bitch in the publicity racket."

Every spring the Fragrance Foundation of New York holds Festival of Fragrance Week. It focuses hype on the fragrance industry and its concerns and, because it arrives at the time spring fever is in the air, it usually gets good media coverage. With this exposure in mind Sally Springsteen approached Cassandra to represent Beautiful Women, a well-known and respected beauty publication, in the festival. Over lunch at the Four Seasons, Sally explained everything to Cassandra.

"Darling, all you have to do is appear at Bloomingdale's perfume counter for one week. Speak on whatever you want, and you'll get coverage in all the media, and get paid a small fortune."

"I'm not sure that is the route I want to take, Sally." Cassandra mused.

"Are you crazy? I know three other psychics who would kill for this sort of exposure." Cassandra looked pensive. "Cassandra, you don't seem to understand. You're getting paid and getting free publicity at the same time. Mabel Fleaman personally endorsed you."

"I hear what you're saying, Sally, but I need time to think about it."

"Don't be a fool, Cassandra. I get paid to think for you in this area, and I have already accepted."

"You what?" Cassandra looked stupefied.

"Listen, I already accepted. If you don't want to do it, I'll get Serena Selznick. They'll be disappointed, but she'll have to do."

"Sally, you know Serena is a fake. Sometimes, I Just don't believe you." Cassandra shook her head in disgust.

"Darling, believe what you want. It's a jungle out there and a girl has to eat. Call me and let me know your answer. You know I can't wait forever." Cassandra looked sullen. "You better listen to me Cassandra Collins; the media doesn't give a shit about whether a psychic is real or not; they believe it's all one big joke anyway. They do it for the ratings and to push newspapers. You can look at all the rags on the newsstand to bear me out. The question is, do you want to go for it or not? Think about it honey." Sally packed her brief case. "I've got to run, don't get up."

Cassandra was in a funk, realizing what Sally said was true. Another moral dilemma. Render to Caesar, she thought. If she did it, Bobby could attend the fragrance ball with her. It would get them coverage in the *Post* – he would love it. People would probably put them in again, making it their third picture this year. Damn, I might as well do it, at least I'm for real and maybe some of the matrons at Bloomies will profit from what I'll say. It may not be the Sermon on the Mount, but it may do someone some good. Cassandra's wheels were spinning; in her own mind she fancied herself as the psychic Joyce Brothers, the pop Normam Vincent Peale, the psychic who cared and who made a difference. Her weekly radio show was already a smash in New York, and there was talk it would eventually be nationwide. So Cassandra compromised one more time, giving in to Sally's demands. She finished her Perrier and motioned to the waiter to bring the check.

Sally made sure that Bloomingdales put an ad in the Sunday Times complete with Cassandra's picture and big. A little paragraph beneath the picture read; 'Internationally acclaimed psychic Cassandra Collins will speak at noon, on Bloomingdales main floor on

Color and Fragrance and the 1980's Woman. All are welcome to listen to Ms. Collins and speak to her on individual problems, brought to you by the editors of *Beautiful Woman* magazine.'

The phone rang all day long. Friends were congratulating her on the Bloomies ad. Even her brothers saw it and called. Cassandra was thrilled. It was a validation for her family; crazy Cassandra was now respectable in the mainstream of American life. Somehow it seemed ironic. Cassandra believed Bloomingdales was the premiere temple of Manhattan where the people worshipped the god of material wealth, and now she was speaking there. Move over St. Patrick's, she thought to herself and laughed.

The day arrived for Cassandra's big day at Bloomingdale's. The limousine from Beautiful Woman Magazine picked up Cassandra along with the publicity director and the women's editor. Both women were very cordial and distant as if they were sharing the car with a relative who was being released from some sort of mental hospital. Cassandra wished that the hard-nosed Sally was there when she needed her. She knew, however, Sally would be orchestrating the commotion at the store. So she made the best of the awkward ride with idle chit chat and girl talk.

The imperious attitude the magazine ladies took with Cassandra even annoyed her more. When Cassandra introduced the women to Sally one of them said, "Cassandra is just so precious, Sally. Now we know why you find her so adorable", as if they were talking about a pampered child star instead of a thirty year old woman. People never knew how to take Cassandra. They were either gushing about her as the next thing to Jesus Christ, or treating her as a leper, a freak, or a combination of both.

The first thing Cassandra noticed was the poster the art department of Bloomingdales had done of her. It was a black and white cardboard mat with her picture on it. Sally was fighting with a salesperson about the position of it. Cassandra was mortified at the scene she was making. Next, the buyer from men's wear objected to where she was to be standing with a microphone, fearing it would cut into his lunchtime business, so there was another huge stink about that. It seemed the buyer of cosmetics and fragrances failed to get prior approval from the floor manager for the placement of

Cassandra; it was a clear case of the right hand not knowing or in this case, even caring what the left hand was doing, so another fracas occurred.

By this time people from the streets were pouring into the fragrance department demanding to talk with, and meet Cassandra, and to receive their souvenir box of complimentary fragrances. What was promised to be a well-orchestrated affair turned into a typical New York mob scene and Cassandra, between the bright lights, confusion, and overpowering smell of the mixture of perfumes and colognes felt she would pass out. She rushed to the ladies lounge where Sally promptly followed.

"What's with you, dear?"

Cassandra replied, "I don't know, I feel sick."

"Listen to me. You better get well real soon because we've got a hell of a lot riding on this appearance, and don't forget we've got five more days of it, so you better get used to it."

Cassandra bristled at the tone in Sally's voice, and her face began to turn red.

"I don't fail to honor my commitments, as you well know Sally, I just need ten minutes to collect myself and I'll be fine."

"Okay by me, as long as you don't

start pulling that diva alert shit on me."

As Sally stormed out Cassandra went into a booth, closed the door to the toilet stall and lost her entire breakfast. As the flushed the toilet, she wished she could dispense with Sally just like her breakfast.

The rest of the week flowed smoothly, Cassandra was calm and poised; the people loved her and she made a fabulous impression. Bobby and his staff stopped over for her last appearance on Saturday afternoon and when she was done speaking they all applauded her. Cassandra was pleased it went so smoothly, and promised herself that in the future she would not let these public appearances unnerve her so much; she would view them as a game and play with the audience and enjoy herself.

A beauty editor who was in the crowd later contacted Cassandra for an article on beauty and fragrance. As a result of the article, Cassandra was approached by a publishing house to do a book. Sally arranged a liaison with a young health and beauty expert, and they put together a psychic beauty and fragrance book. Cassandra was booked on radio and television talk shows promoting the book, which became, with Sally's hype, a national bestseller.

With her increasing success, and her business flourishing, another problem surfaced that was to plague Cassandra for the rest of her life. When people became aware of her fantastic gift of seeing into the future they sought her advice on every minute question. She didn't mind her closest friends asking her, in fact, she loved helping them, but it became annoying for her to be questioned about every little thing. She was too thin-skinned to avoid helping people in pain, but the increasing demands on her energy became a drain.

One day talking with Sally, Cassandra complained about the people draining her, and Sally gave her advice, "Honey, if they are not feeding you or fucking you, forget them. You can't dance at ten weddings, and you'll kill yourself if you try." Sally's advice rang true, but Cassandra still felt guilty when she couldn't be all things to all people.

Chapter Thirty One

One lovely spring evening after a candlelight dinner at the Village Green Restaurant on Greenwich Village's Hudson Street, Cassandra and Bobby decided to walk back to his loft in Chelsea. Bobby bought Cassandra a rose from a sidewalk vendor.

"For you, my dear", he said, looking into her eyes." Cassandra smiled; in her mind's eye she was seeing peaceful scenes of the shore in summertime.

"Cassandra, you look far away, darling. A penny for your thoughts?"

"Oh, I was just thinking of the beach. In a few weeks it will be time for planning the summer, and I was longing for the ocean again."

"Like John Masefield's *Sea Fever*?"

"Yes, I must go down to the sea again..."

"I want you to spend the summer with me in the Pines."

Cassandra stopped walking and looked at Bobby. "Do you really mean it?"

"Of course, silly. I want us to spend the summer together. I couldn't imagine you not being with me at the beach in summertime. You can come out with me Memorial Day weekend. I'm planning a party to kickoff the season and I want you with me, by my side." Cassandra had tears come into her eyes.

"I'd love to Bobby. It sounds so wonderful."

Cassandra was raised on Long Island and her family always spent the summers in the Hamptons where they owned their own home. Her two brothers each built their own homes where they went every summer with their wives and children. Cassandra was always welcome there, but she hadn't spent a whole summer at the beach in many years, and she was excited as a schoolgirl with the prospect of a summer vacation.

And to spend it with Bobby; now she was certain of his love.

Cassandra began to trust the relationship and began to mellow. She thought to herself, "Maybe I'm not cursed in love after all." That night for the first time making love she didn't see Peter's face, and for that she was grateful.

The weeks before, setting up housekeeping in Fire Island, just flew by. Cassandra had her Sunday night radio program and the weekly appearance on the morning television show. She realized she would have to spend at least two days in the city. Sally's incessant harping on the matter didn't help but she could manage to be on Fire Island with Bobby the rest of the week. She wouldn't see any Manhattan clients for the summer; instead she would read for the people on the island three afternoons a week and the other time she would have totally free to swim, read, relax, and enjoy life. The summer held real promise.

The Pines is a community on Fire Island that attracts the wealthiest and best known of the gay elite culture of New York. Bobby Daniels was no stranger to this incredible world of fantasy and money. Quite the contrary, he was one of its premiere stars. Each year, he helped with the different charity shows for the fire department, the preservation league, and most recently, the AIDS Benefit.

Bobby owned a huge waterfront home on the Harbor side of the Pines. It was widely rumored, according to the Santeria Religion, the protecting water spirit of the harbor lived on his property. The house was a fantastic creation in every aspect; there was a view of the harbor and bay from every window. The main part of the house had a huge cathedral ceiling; the master bath had a jacuzzi and sauna, and outside on the grounds overlooking the bay was a huge heated swimming pool. Bobby built a gazebo where, on cool evenings you could sleep outside and look up at the stars. He built the house in 1968 for a little over $95,000 and it was worth, by today's standards, well over a million and a half. It was to this wood and glass palace

Cassandra was brought to on Memorial Day to begin the summer season.

All the queens were holding their breath to find out who the lucky one was to share Bobby's bed and his wonderful summer home. They were shocked to learn it was the psychic, Cassandra Collins. It had been long bantered about in the dishy gay circles that Bobby was a "switch-hitter," but no one could recall in recent memory his ever escorting a woman to the island. Of course, he took up-and-coming starlets to premieres, but the Pines was a private place where you could be yourself, and the presence of Cassandra was noticed as something out of the ordinary.

The community welcomed Cassandra with open arms, if not a sense of amazement, and a little skepticism. Although her reputation as a fine psychic was already well established, Bobby used his powers of persuasion to see that all his friends had readings by her. By the end of their first summer together on the island, Cassandra had read for everyone of note.

They all came to understand why Bobby adored her so. She wasn't a gold digger or star fucker, and she was wealthy in her own right.

She was a dedicated counselor, and by the end of the season a growing respect for both Bobby and Cassandra was evidenced by the deference accorded them, like a minister and his wife.

The only thing Bobby failed to realize was the provincial smallness of the Pines, so the indiscretions he could easily hide in Manhattan were obviously out in the open at the Pines. Cassandra wasn't blind to Bobby's sudden disappearances, but she overlooked them as a mother overlooks the faults of a beloved child. To everyone's amazement, the relationship worked, and Bobby and Cassandra seemed more and more in love each day.

Bobby would only rarely go back into the city to attend to business. He trusted Helen DeVito to handle all his business affairs, and during July and August, Helen spent every weekend at the beach house with Cassandra and Bobby. He had one of the bedrooms set up as a studio and if anyone needed him for a fitting or a consultation they could damn well fly out on the seaplane from Manhattan to see him. Bobby had worked long and hard over the years to achieve what he had, so his attitude was "Fuck them if they can't take a joke."

Cassandra learned a lot from Bobby's attitude toward life. He wasn't born with a silver spoon in his mouth like she was, but he enjoyed life with a gusto she never had. It was his love of life she loved most about Bobby. He was like a little boy, enthused over everything. Bobby was a good balance for Cassandra, who lived in a fantasy world half the time. For the first time since she was a little girl; she began to really let go and enjoy life to the fullest. Bobby let none of the world's artificial barriers impose on his joy. His overflowing love of life rubbed off to good effect on Cassandra.

Bobby was a people person and hated to be alone. Although he wasn't always the best judge of character, he had no trouble taking care of himself. Because he genuinely loved people, he overlooked their flaws. Cassandra, on the other hand, was very careful about whom she let into her world. She needed much alone time to meditate and recover her energy after being with people for any period of time.

Bobby loved to go dancing at all hours, but Cassandra couldn't stand loud music. She would stay out on the deck looking at the stars, playing her Seapeace tape by Georgia Kelly on her Walkman, while the loud disco music filled the air. Cassandra was the only person Bobby ever took to "tea" at the Blue Whale who wasn't impressed. Bobby left Cassandra at home when he wanted to make the "scene", and she never objected to his going. It was the first relationship he had ever experienced where he had freedom. All the others were afraid of losing him and clung until he felt suffocated and he wound up leaving them, but not Cassandra. She was strangely content and had a serenity about her Bobby found totally reassuring.

Although they were opposite in so many ways they were alike in that they were both sincere, good, and successful people. Bobby taught Cassandra to disco so that by the end of the summer, when on occasion she did want to accompany him, she became a fine dancer. She, on the other hand taught him to meditate twice a day. He never before had known inner peace, except after the ecstasy of intercourse. Each made significant inroads into the other's life over the course of the summer.

Chapter Thirty Two

When the summer was over, Bobby and Cassandra went back to Manhattan to resume the normal pattern of their lives. They usually spent weekends together, but during the week they kept their lives apart, linking two or three times a day by phone. Cassandra knew during this time that Bobby was involved with a dancer from one of the Broadway shows he designed the costumes for, but it didn't bother her as long as she knew he was happy.

She was satisfied spending the weekends with him but, as the year wore on, their love decreased to kissing and cuddling, and although sometimes she longed for more, she was happy just to be with him and be part of his life. Bobby's dancer boyfriend provided the sexual release he so desperately craved and she gave him the affection he longed for otherwise. Unusual as their relationship was, it worked.

The months went by and before long Christmas season was upon them. Bobby decided to fly home to England for the holidays to spend with his family, as he did every year, so Cassandra had to make up her mind what to do. She realized Bobby would love to take her home to meet his family, but she didn't feel right about it. Going to the Pines was one thing, but meeting someone's family at the holidays was another. She declined and decided to spend the time with her brothers and their families on Long Island, as she had done every year. Then she would spend the week after Christmas in St. Croix, as usual. Alone again.

Time and time again St. Croix proved to be a healing experience for Cassandra. She managed not to feel so alone in the sunny climate with her old friends who for various reasons were also exiled from the mainland at holiday time. Her artistic tendencies surfaced as she brought her watercolors and painted to her heart's content. She managed to read a few bestsellers she had neglected since summer, and got a really good rest.

One night, she was awakened by a horrible nightmare. In the dream she saw a beautiful woman kiss Bobby on the mouth, and when the woman turned around, it was a drag queen with blood gushing out of his mouth. Cassandra woke up shaking. She calmed herself down, trying to explain it away as an anxiety dream, and managed to fall back to sleep again, but once asleep, she saw herself dressed in black reading a copy of the *New York Post*. The headline read "Top designer dead of dreaded gay plague." She saw Bobby's picture on the front page and again awakened this time totally terror stricken.

She immediately called New York, but when she finally reached Bobby's line, all she got was his answering machine. Of course, she realized he was still with his family in England. She hoped somehow with the knowledge of the dream she could somehow alter the future. She remembered reading about AIDS and how 75% of its victims were gay or bisexual men. She felt her blood run cold. Thank God they hadn't slept together in months.

She thought about Bobby. Recently he had lost some weight and he did have a dry cough, but she never put two and two together. Then she remembered his hush-hush visits to the dermatologist. Maybe that was why he wasn't sleeping with her for fear he would become her angel of death. Cassandra vowed to confront him with her fears when she returned to New York and he returned from England.

When she got back to Manhattan, Cassandra called Helen DeVito. "Helen, it's Cassandra. Happy New Year, dear. Is Bobby back?"

"Hi, Doll Face. Yes he is. He's with a client, I'll have him call you when he's through. How were the Islands?"

"Lovely, as usual. Maybe I'll stop by and surprise him."

Helen was unusually quiet. "Sure, that would be fine. See you later."

"Good-bye." As Cassandra hung up the receiver, she realized she wasn't being paranoid; something was wrong, and Helen knew it.

Cassandra wasn't ready for the shock when she saw Bobby. It had only been a little over three weeks since they had been together, and she wasn't prepared for the change in his appearance. He was swollen, his eyes looking like slants in a bizarre pumpkin face.

He was happy to see her, but as he hugged her, he pointedly avoided kissing her.

"Darling, Happy New Year. The doctor has shot me up with cortisone and I'm all swollen."

"Bobby, you look awful, how are you feeling?" Tears came to Cassandra's eyes.

"I'm feeling fine. The doctor says I have some allergy in my blood, but that I'll be just fine." He gave Cassandra his usual charming smile.

"So how was St. Croix?"

"St. Croix was fine, but I missed you, of

course. I kept thinking about you in England with your family, and was hoping you were having a good time."

"The family was fine, but I wasn't feeling too chipper. Otherwise, it was a good holiday."

Cassandra noticed a cloud come over Bobby's face.

"Bobby, while I was away I dreamed about you being very ill, and I couldn't stand the thought. How are you really?"

Bobby looked perplexed. what was your dream about, Cass? The truth, cannon."

Cassandra's eyes were transparent, looking into them he knew she had dreamed of his secret; it was no use trying to hide any longer.

"Bobby, I dreamed you had that awful disease, AIDS. Tell me I'm paranoid or something. Please."

"Cassandra, sit down." He pulled her over to the large antique divan. "I've never lied to you, and don't intend to start now. Dr. Green made a positive identification for Acquired Immune Deficiency Syndrome — AIDS. I was going to tell you as soon as I could accept it myself. Since I've found out I haven't been able to eat or sleep." He began to sob. "Cass, I'm afraid. I'm scared out of my mind."

She held him and he cried in her arms like a lost little boy. Cassandra cried, too. Rocking him in her arms, knowing the fate that was too horrible to discuss. She just held him close to her breast and prayed.

Chapter Thirty Three

Only two weeks after his diagnosis with AIDS, Bobby's life was snuffed out by Pneumocystis Carinii pneumonia. The doctor told him he would recover with the help of some new, powerful antibiotics, but he was wrong. The most alive and happy person Cassandra had ever know never left St. Vincent's Hospital.

As Bobby drifted in and out of a feverish coma, Cassandra spent every waking moment at his bedside helplessly waiting as his life force ebbed. She felt him slipping away, so she held his hand and prayed.

Only she and Helen De Vito knew he was hospitalized. His clients and family members were told by Bobby that he was in the Orient on a buying trip so no one was suspicious of his absence from the business. Bobby wanted his diagnosis to remain a secret from the media.

On the thirteenth day of his hospital stay, Bobby drew his last breath. The sweet young nurse in attendance hugged Cassandra's shoulders. "There is nothing more for you to do, Miss Collins. Go home and get some sleep."

She helped Cassandra up from Bobby's bedside. Cassandra couldn't cry. She had wept so much in the past few days there were no tears left to shed. She leaned over Bobby and kissed his angelic face one more time. "Good night, sweet prince."

Cassandra was desolate. Without Bobby, nothing would be the same. Voices inside her head jarred her senses. She kept seeing Dr. Green's face, telling her, to "Consider yourself lucky, Miss Collins. You tested negative for the virus. By using condoms and spermicide you were protected from infection."

Consider herself lucky? All the men she ever cared about were taken from her. It was almost like the Universe was laughing at a horrible joke. Was she kissed by the gods or cursed by them? In her grief and pain she began to wonder.

She wished that somehow she had given Bobby the child he always wanted. One with his beautiful cherubic face and angelic little laugh. Was she really a selfish bitch? Her mind was racked with guilt, anger, rage, and pain. She was exhausted from the two week vigil at his deathbed. Praying with all her soul that the angel of death would somehow pass him by, but knowing in her heart his fate was sealed. Thinking about it made her want to scream.

She wandered out of the hospital into the street. It was pouring rain and she had neglected to bring an umbrella or wear the Burberry slicker Bobby had bought her a few months before in London. She frantically looked around for a cab to take her far away from the hospital with its sad memories

A yellow checker cab pulled up to the front of the hospital to let off an elderly man. The cab's light was off, indicating he was off duty, but when the driver saw Cassandra's distressed state he called out to her, "Where do you want to go, Lady?"

She rushed over to the cab, "To St. Patrick's."

"Okay. Get in. You must need to pray pretty bad to be out in this weather."

Cassandra nodded in agreement as the driver sped across town in the teaming rain and up Fifth Avenue to the Gothic cathedral. Cassandra pulled a fifty out of her pocket book and didn't wait for change.

The driver called back to her. "Hey, lady. Thanks. I hope things work out for you."

But Cassandra didn't look back. She raced up the steps of the church and opened the heavy doors to the sanctuary.

Walking down the long candlelit side aisle, she thought of all the lonely times she had sought refuge at the altar of the Blessed Mother; it her grandmother's favorite place to pray.

She had come here after breaking up with Peter and losing the baby on her return to New York fourteen years before. And two years ago, after her breakup with Philip Kingston. How many more times would she have to be reduced to this state by the loss of a man?

As Cassandra got down on her knees and prayed, she gazed at the statue intently. An unearthly light seemed to penetrate the air. She felt a warmth flood over her body, and heard a small, reassuring voice whisper in her ear, "Cry no more daughter of Jerusalem. Your tears have not been shed in vain."

Cassandra closed her eyes. The smell of roses was overwhelming. She felt transported to another time and place. She was shown a house on a hill. In her mind's eye, she entered the house and saw a beautiful crystal chandelier in a hallway with a black and white marble floor. She felt as if she were in a waking dream, like Dorothy stepping out of her house into the enchanted gardens of Oz.

She came back to her senses, having no idea how much time had passed. She was cold, but perspiration was pouring off her body. Never before had she experienced so powerful a vision. Tears of joy coursed down her face as she gave thanks for being shown her new path.

It was still raining as Cassandra left the church. She realized she didn't have her umbrella or raincoat, but she didn't care. Still feeling warmly enveloped by the feeling of her vision, she began walking up Fifth Avenue. The rain soaking into her skin felt good.

On impluse she decided to stop and buy a pack of cigarettes when she spied a picture of Philip and Mrs. Kingston on the cover of *Town and Country*. She picked up the magazine and paid for it with her cigarettes.

Arriving home, Cassandra shed her soaking clothes in the foyer, and tossed the magazine by the door. She made her way into the bathroom and turned on the gold dolphin spigots to her large marble tub, filling it with warm water. She put on a silk robe and went into the kitchen to brew herself a cup of Sleepytime herb tea.

Grabbing the magazine from the floor, anxious to read the article about Philip, she noticed it was opened to an advertisement for a house. Cassandra couldn't believe her eyes. It was the house she had just seen in her vision.

The ad, with a large picture read,

"North Carolina Estate. Five acres on scenic Lake Wylie, five bedrooms, heated pool, views from every window. $650,000.00. Principals only."

Cassandra removed her robe, and sunk into the warm bath. She knew she wasn't dreaming. After the funeral, she would visit the house in North Carolina. It seemed so ironic. Just as one world was collapsing, a better one was being born.

Chapter Thirty Four

Events transpired so quickly Cassandra felt as if she were in a daze. Not since the death of her grandmother many years before had she known such turmoil. She notified Bobby's family in England of his passing, and they had to make funeral arrangements. The phone rang off the hook as mutual friends wanted to find out how she was faring and what plans she was making for the funeral. If it weren't for Helen de Vito, Danny and Megan, she would have totally lost her mind.

The press was turning Bobby's death into the media event of the year. He had dressed seven of the last ten Academy Award winners and all of them had their secretaries call for information of the funeral. Sally Springsteen was attempting to capitalize on the publicity, and Cassandra was revolted. She felt the funeral should be carried out with dignity, but she also knew Bobby would love all the show business people making a fuss over his departure; she also knew he wanted to make his final exit in style.

In Bobby's will he specified he wanted to be laid out in Campbell's Funeral Home, where his beloved Judy Garland's wake was held. The event turned out to be a veritable nightmare for Cassandra.

Outside the funeral home the mourners were lined up three people deep. Getting out of the car the funeral home sent for her, Cassandra was beseiged by photographers and reporters. The paparazzi turned Bobby's wake into a three ring circus with the omnivorous Sally Springsteen as the ringmaster.

As each limousine pulled up to the funeral home, Sally was outside telling all the photographers who each one was, as if she were announcing the Academy Awards. Broadway stars, recording artists, movie stars, television personalities, it was a "Who's Who" of the glitteratti of New York and L.A. Several well known stars flew in from the coast just to be pall bearers.

Many of them loved Bobby, as did Cassandra. They would sorely miss his boyish charm, and bright wit, but others just came to be seen and get a mention in the evening news. Cassandra couldn't believe even death couldn't be handled with dignity by Sally. She made up her mind that after the funeral, Sally was getting the ax once and for all.

Cassandra rode to the cemetery in the front car with Bobby's widowed mother, a pleasant English woman in her early seventies. His sister and her husband rode in the second car with their relatives who flew in from England for the funeral. In the third car were Helen DeVito and a few members of Bobby's staff. The ride up to the cemetery in Westchester was uneventful, and the ceremony conducted by an old Episcopal priest was short. He said a few words about Bobby's life and read the 23rd Psalm, Bobby's favorite prayer.

Riding back to the city, Cassandra was at peace. She loved Bobby, but after her vision in St. Patrick's she could let him go. What she couldn't let go of were the bad feelings toward the vipers at the funeral; the people who went just to gape at the mourners. She felt they were a bunch of ghouls. Her mind flashed back to Joe Di Maggio's handling of Marilyn Monroe's funeral. She suddenly understood why he refused to let the Hollywood crowd attend.

Death deserved to have a dignity of its own, no matter how famous or celebrated one is in life.Cassandra was made painfully aware of the negative aspects of the fame Bobby craved and ultimately attained, and how meaningless it was when faced with the inevitability of death. Cassandra thought back to her grandmother saying over and over again, "No one ever gets out of this life alive."

After the funeral, Cassandra wandered alone down to Karl Schurz Park. She loved sitting on the promenade watching the boats go by, and she secretly enjoyed seeing the nannies and governesses pushing their young charges around in the carriages. Cassandra always loved children, and in her heart hoped she would have some. The idea of motherhood appealed to her, as she had a great deal of love to shower upon a child.

Nothing would give her greater pleasure. She didn't ever want to stop helping people with her counseling, but how nice it would be to have her own family. She remembered the happy days sitting in the kitchen with her grandmother while she was baking bread and pies and she would do her lessons at the great oak table. She also remembered the holidays on Long Island with her brothers and the huge Christmas tree with the gifts piled at its foot.

In her heart she longed for these things. Things success hadn't brought her, and the man who went with them. She wondered if she would ever attain her dream in New York. She asked for a sign from heaven on what to do. Lost in a dream world of her own, she felt something wet and awful strike her on the forehead. Bird shit. She didn't believe it. My God. Ask and you shall receive. She had the impulse to laugh and to scream at the same time.

She searched for her bag to find a hankie, and realized she had left it at home. She went up to a lady and asked for a tissue and the woman avoided her as if she were a crazed bag lady. No one recognized her with her sunglasses and Missoni scarf tied over her fabulous auburn hair, but now with the bird crap on her head, the people thought she was crazy. After the third person she approached shunned her, Cassandra grabbed a leaf off a bush and wiped the excrement from her forehead. My God, no one was there to help her, it was a scene out of a surrealistic nightmare, but it was actually happening to her.

Her mind was made up. She would leave New York. This was too real to be accidental. The universe had a strange way of letting one know what was up. Cassandra had to be literally hit in the head to realize her life in New York was shit, and although it was fertilizer, she would choose to grow elsewhere.

A week after the funeral, Cassandra received a call to go down to Roland Taylor's office for the reading of Bobby's will. She dressed simply in a gray crepe de chine dress with a single strand of pearls. She pulled her hair back into a chignon and wore no makeup. She just wanted to get the reading behind her and forget about it.

She was afraid all the bad memories of the last two weeks would surface. She only wanted to remember the good times; the summer at the Pines, their first romantic dinner in the loft, and the fabulous weekends they spent together. All the other things she intended to blot out of her mind forever.

Cassandra took a cab to the large office between Lexington and Third Avenues. She took the elevator up to a paneled office and was informed by the very chic, young black secretary to have a seat Cassandra noticed Alice Duncan and her photographer husband, Bill Balley,were seated waiting to see Ronald's partner and literary agent Ben Shanely. She picked up a *People* magazine and started to read, her mind wandering far away.

The secretary beckoned her, "Miss Collins, Mr. Taylor is ready to see you."

Cassandra absentmindedly put the magazine down and walked over to Roland Taylor.

"Hello Miss Gollins. I hope this will be as painless as possible."

Cassandra wondered why she was the only one present, but she said, "Thank you, Mr. Taylor."

Roland Taylor was a big man, and very regal looking. He was a graduate of Harvard law and was an amatuer thespian at school. His love of the theater brought him to New York, where he set up his law practice. After several years he decided to specialize in entertainment law, and he now represented many of the best actors, directors, and producers. Bobby had always gone for the biggest and the best, so picking Roland Taylor was true to his style.

He sat down behind his oak desk. The walls were covered with pictures taken of him with celebrities from every area of showbusiness for the last twenty years. Cassandra looked and him and listened.

"Bobby and I were friends as I'm sure you know, Miss Collins. He asked that only you be present when his will was read."

Cassandra nodded quietly as Roland proceeded to read the will. All the cash in his accounts was to be divided among his family. The half million he left, would set them up fairly well. The business and loft were left to Helen DeVito for all the years of loyal service she gave to him. He left all his personal effects and the beach house at the Pines to Cassandra.

Tears welled up in Cassandra's eyes. Bobby made certain their idyllic summer would never be forgotten. Even after death he knew how to make things beautiful. In her mind's eye, she could see him now as he was last summer, lean and tan, blessed by the sun's rays, smiling and forever young.

Chapter Thirty Five

It was late April and the season at the Pines hadn't yet begun. Cassandra loved the quiet of the beach house before the tourists started arriving at Memorial Day with the big kick-off parties to start the season. With Bobby gone, this year there would be no party at her house. She couldn't bring herself to do it; she was still on the mend. She came out to relax and to forget New York. Megan Monroe was the only friend she had out to the house, preferring to be alone the rest of the time. She was in the process of making some very heavy decisions and she knew Megan was sensitive enough to understand what she was feeling deep in her heart.

The *Seapeace* tape was playing softly in

the background. Cassandra brought her music out to the Pines; she couldn't bear the idea of any of the disco records from Bobby's enormous record collection. In fact, whenever she heard any disco music she connected in her mind with his death.

Megan stirred in her bed in the other room. While the sun was coming up over the ocean, dawn was breaking in all its glory. Megan crept into the bathroom and looked at the ocean sparking with the wind making whitecaps on the top of the waves. She went into the living room and found Cassandra drinking her espresso, staring out at the water.

"Good morning." Megan said cheerfully.

Cassandra turned, "Hi, hon. Did you sleep well?"

"Better than I have in months. This place is more peaceful than anywhere I visited in India. You really have everything, Cass."

"Do I now? Let me see." Cassandra said joking.

"Oh, you know what I mean. Look at it this way. I spend six months going to India on a spiritual journey, and all I see are people shitting in the streets, corpses being burned on funeral pyres, hear goddamn bicycle bells, get bitten by bloodsucking mosquitoes, and feel the aura of overpowering poverty. What a paradox for such a spiritual nation. The only peace I had during the whole trip was the one night of sleeping on the Ganges with an American photojournalist friend who I ran into over there with a rented houseboat. And here you have it all."

"You've never been out to the Pines when it wasn't wild, have you?"

"No, and I couldn't imagine how quiet it could be."

"Yes, there is a power in silence, isn't there?" Asking the question rhetorically. "Something to think about. You know, Megan, I've been doing a lot of thinking out here. I've decided to give up the weekly astrology spot on the network."

"You have?"

"Yes. I just can't do sun sign astrology any more and feel comfortable with it. I try to inject positive thought and spiritual values into it as much as I can, but it is too draining, and keeping it good and maintaining my integrity is just getting to be too much of a drain."

Megan shifted, realizing that this was to be a monologue. Cassandra was pouring her heart out, and Megan had never seen her in this light before. She was fascinated.

"I have had a great deal more revelations since Bobby died. Coming out of the hospital one night, I couldn't go home so I went over to the Regency to see *Gone With the Wind*. I related so much to Scarlett after the war, when she had lost everything in Atlanta and went back to Tara. I realized that in some ways this house here was Bobby's Tara, not mine."

"What are you going to do?"

"I don't exactly know. I had a vision in St. Patrick's of a beautiful country home, and then I saw the identical house advertised in *Town and Country*."

"That doesn't surprise me."

"Nor me, either. I am going to North Carolina to look at it."

"All fine and good, but what will you do once you get there?"

"Well, I know for sure I'm not going to do a fade out on the hill overlooking Tara with Max Steiner's music blaring in the background. I'll do my counseling wherever I go. I've thought about writing an autobiographical novel, a disguised one of course."

"Knowing your life it will be a doozie." Megan smiled.

"You're right, it will be. It's funny, Megan, but the happiest times of my life, besides the few months with Peter in Vermont, and the good times with Phil and Bobby are the alone times."

"Well, in that case I'll be going." Megan made a mock motion to get up.

"Sit down, silly, and listen. What I've always sought in life was a kind of balance. Balance of my work and life.When I was christened, my father engraved on my baby cup, "May your life be kissed by the gods." All my life it has haunted me like some kind of prophecy or curse. I want nothing but the best, but not just in a material way. I've had it with the fame, glitz and bullshit. I want to do a good day's work and spend the evening curled in front of the fireplace with the man I love, and, God willing, with a couple of kids.

That is all I ever wanted. And I feel like time is running out, and I don't believe I'll ever find it in New York either. Every night there is a more fabulous opening, soiree, or party. It's glamorous, but I need more than glamour, I need real . . . Here, I feel too fragmented." She paused to sip her espresso.

"The last present Bobby gave me before he died was a gray Marilyn Monroe T-shirt with the saying, "Victim of Glamour," spelled out in little barbiturate tablets. Well, I deserve more. I mean, Jesus Christ, here I am almost 34 and she was dead at 36."

"Aren't we getting a little heavy?" Megan tried to inject some humor.

"No, I mean when I'm old, I want more than to have been on the cover of *People* magazine. You know what I mean?"

"I hear you."

"I mean besides my brothers, you, Danny, and Richardson, who really gives a damn?"

"Cassandra, have some more espresso. I know it will all work out, you'll see."

"Now who's the counselor?" She smiled at Megan, as a tear rolled down her face.

Chapter Thirty Six

Not wanting to be out at the Pines on Memorial Day weekend, Cassandra flew down to North Carolina to see the estate she saw in her vision at St. Patrick's and advertised in *Town and Country*. The house was several miles outside of the Charlotte, a booming southern city on the border between North and South Carolina. Cassandra had made an appointment by telephone with the real estate agent handling the property and took a cab to the realtor's office after she settled in a local hotel.

Cassandra waited in the office for the real estate agent to gather up her things. She was a divorced woman in her fifties, well put together, with gray hair impeccably coiffed, even if it was in a rather outdated style, wearing a conservative black suit with silk blouse. Cassandra intuitively felt this woman was a top agent, knowing her business and able to size up clients immediately. They formed an instant rapport, and Cassandra knew this woman was intent on selling her the house.

"Well, I'm all ready." She said smiling.

"Here are the details on the house." She handed Cassandra the listing sheet of the estate, the amount of land, the size of the home, the tax value and all pertinent information resulting to the purchase. Cassandra saw the price and she couldn't believe it was so low, $650,000. If this was in New York or Connecticut it would be well over two million dollars. The woman would faint when Cassandra paid cash for it. She would sell the Fire Island home at the at the end of the season for a cool million and have the rest of her money to play with. Yes, this was going to be her freedom from New York and she would start her new life here.

Life looked good, and she was going to get her piece of the pie. She would love the South, its people, its ways and like Mame she would conquer their hearts. Cassandra believed the vision of the home was meant for her life to take on a new direction, she was confident all would be well.

As they drove up to the home, Cassandra was not prepared for what she saw. The house was magnificent, beautiful beyond her wildest dreams. Her heart began to race as they drove up the driveway with its oak covered trees shading the winding drive.

The house was an immense two story Georgian colonial, complete with columns on the wrap around front porch. It was perched on a hill in the foothills of the Appalachian Range overlooking Lake Wylie. The back of the house had a tennis court, jacuzzi, and large heated swimming pool surrounded by a blue slate patio with potted fruit trees and flowers. The estate was well situated on five acres and every room in the house had a view of the lake. Cassandra was unable to mask her excitement from the realtor as they went inside the house.

The owner had already been transferred to New York by the large textile manufacturing firm he was vice president of, and Cassandra wondered if he had already bought something else in Long Island or Westchester. The house was empty, and Cassandra considered this to be a good omen.

The circle seemed complete, it was just a matter of formality in her mind to seal the deal. After the grand tour of the house, Cassandra made an offer of $550,000 for the house. The real estate agent phoned the owner and within a half hour they negotiated a compromise price of $600,000 even. Cassandra was in love with the home, and in her mind began furnishing it.

Two months later, Cassandra moved into the house and immediately felt right at home in North Carolina. She loved the house with its immense size, and its feeling of openness and light.

Cassandra's study was done in beautiful Chinese fabric and had the feeling of an Oriental Princess' sitting room. Cassandra spent her days fixing the house to her idea of perfection and lost track of time. Stress seemed to melt away day by day until she realized once again what peace of mind was really about.

Away from the city and its enormous pressures, life began to take on a quality of security and happiness, similar to her childhood days on Long Island with her grandmother. Cassandra once again began to play the piano and paint. Her creativity bloomed. After living in her new home for six months, she looked into the mirror over her fireplace and was stunned. It seemed as if the years had melted away. She looked like she did when she was a student in Vermont. Her skin glowed without makeup and her face was unlined from inner serenity that the days she spent at Elizabeth Arden's succeeded in camouflaging, but were unable to erase. These were good days for Cassandra, and she didn't see any reason to change them.

The calls from New York became less and less, and she felt as if only the few people who mattered were with her.

One afternoon after a deep meditation, the phone rang, and Cassandra answered it, feeling it to be an important call.

"Hello."

"Cassandra, it's Ethel Mason. How is it going down there?" Ethel was the literary agent who sold her beauty book.

"Fine, or should I say better and better."

"Good, dear. Listen, have you thought any more about that novel, darling? I was having lunch yesterday with the editor at St. Martin's and she wanted to know if you had written a synopis yet."

"No, I haven't even given it a thought but thanks for asking."

They proceeded to chit chat about the news and the dish and when Cassandra got off the phone she thought to herself, maybe she would try to sit down and see what would happen at the typewriter. It was pure magic; the words and phrases flew down by themselves, and the plot was already there. She would write a roman-a-clef about her own life. If anyone had a story to tell, it was Cassandra. Who, after all would believe it anyway?

Cassandra fell into a routine very easily. Every day after her morning exercise, she'd shower and go for a swim in the pool. After meditating for twenty minutes, she would sit at her typewriter with a pot of herb tea, and a granola bar. She'd work for two hours, break for lunch, and nap for half an hour, then work again until sundown. She lived like a nun, disciplined for six months until the rough draft was completed. She mailed Ethel a xeroxed copy and within three weeks, even before corrections, it was sold.

Chapter Thirty Seven

The publishing house that took Cassandra's novel was putting a huge promotional budget behind it which meant Cassandra would have to go, once again, on the infamous book tour. In some ways, she was looking forward to it. She had been living in North Carolina for over a year, and it would do her good to get out of the area and circulate again. She was even looking forward to visiting New York and seeing some of her old friends.

The publicist booked her on all the major television talk shows, every radio show imaginable, and set up interviews with all the women's magazines. It was ironic that Cassandra, who had all good intentions of retiring from the limelight, found herself more in focus than before. She believed in the novel with all her heart. It was her story, however disguised, and she was going to do all in her power to see it was a smashing success.

Already the bookclubs had ordered it for their spring lists, and the first printing was 100,000, an extremely large printing for a first novel. The publishers knew they had a best seller on their hands, and the greatest drawing card for the book was Cassandra herself.

Many novelists did not interview well, or take care of their appearance, but here was Cassandra, every bit as beautiful as a movie star, bright, talented, and psychic. An incredible combination, and her publicist knew it.

It was already rumored that the bids for movie rights were starting at a half million, and the paperback rights were expected to go for well over a million. It was to Cassandra's credit she didn't let any of the hoopla surrounding the novel go to her head. She simply had something to say, and she said it. The fact that everyone was eager to read it was fine with her, but she no longer lived to seek others approval.

Cassandra was pleased to learn she was booked on the *Phil Donahue Show*. She made it a point to watch this charismatic and sensitive host whenever she could. He was the one person she felt would not treat her as a freak, and who would get to the heart of the book, the inner world of the psychic's mind.

It was well known in the industry that one appearance on Donohue could mean the difference of 50,000 copies in hardcover alone.

Dr. Peter Brown, professor of psychiatry at Chicago's Downtown Medical School, was sitting in his office reading the daily paper as a break from his teaching duties and heavy client load. He had just finished reviewing the galleys for his first book on past life regressions, and how they aided the therapy of highly disturbed clients with psychosomatic health problems. He knew the book was good, and he expected to make a few ripples in the medical community.

He picked up the paper to look at the evening's television listings, his one escape from the day's pressures. His eyes chanced upon the advertisement for a Donohue taping. The ad read: *"Phil Donohue will interview Cassandra Collins, well known psychic astrologer, and novelist on his show Thursday."* A picture of Cassandra accompanied the article.

Peter couldn't believe his eyes. Cassandra, the only woman he ever loved, here in Chicago. My God, what did this mean? He would have told his clients about synchronicity, having just thought of her this morning, but that was nothing new because he thought of her every morning, noon, and night for the past fourteen years.

All his psychoanalysis and therapy had not been able to erase her from his consciousness. He had given up hope of even trying, but now the opportunity of a lifetime appeared. Many times he had seen that when patients confronted fears, they vanished. Well, he had enough already. He would take his own medicine and finally lay his ghost to rest. He would confront Cassandra and free himself from the self-imposed prison he constructed for himself all these years.

Oh, he had slept with other women from time to time, but no one compared with Cassandra. He felt there would never be another woman to fill her place, but to continue this way was madness. He would exorcise her from his soul and finally get on with his life he put on hold years ago in Vermont.

Cassandra was certain she was well rested and looking her best for the guest appearance. The publishing house flew in their publicist, Deanna Rose, a real lady, quite a contrast to Sally Springsteen. Cassandra shuddered whenever she thought of that woman.

Deanna was a dabbler in astrology and the occult, so was a little bit in awe of Cassandra. Because Deanna was incredibly beautiful, and had a good position at the publishing house, she could relate to Cassandra as an equal. In fact, they became good friends.

They were put up in the best hotels and treated royally. Cassandra had a little stage fright, not because of the questions Donahue would ask, but a vague uneasiness, coming from the audience participation.

She tried talking herself out of the anxiety, but she had a psychic premonition it had nothing to do with nerves. It was more a women's intuition. This show would change her life in some dramatic way. It all seemed silly, really, because she couldn't figure out how, but nevertheless, trouper that she was, the show must go on. Cassandra braced herself, put on her best face, and walked from the green room onto the set. She sensed that Donahue liked her immediately, so she relaxed and sat down to talk with him, forgetting the audience and the camera. She was hot and she knew it.

She fielded the questions like a pro and could see out of the corner of her eye that Deanna was jubilant. The first part of the show went beautifully. Cassandra explained her work as plainly as she could, answering all sorts of detailed questions on clairvoyance and prophecy.

Donahue was impressed with her sincerity, and he had every reason to be. When he asked her about the parallels between her own life and the novel, Cassandra had to be very careful, since it was almost drawn directly from her life, she had changed names, places, and whatever to disguise identities so people wouldn't get hurt, for her intention in writing the novel was more cathartic than anything. She was not lashing out to do damage, but looking at her life from the perspective of art, to get a better handle on her own sense of who she was and where she belonged in the world.

The audience was made up of many different people, asking her questions about political figures, themselves, the economy, and different celebrities. She almost stopped dead in her tracks, she thought she saw a ghost. The next man to ask a question was Peter Brown. A chill went through Cassandra. It was as if all her lives were converging at one point in time, and this was the moment. Part of her mind listened to the question.

"What will be the future of parapsychology in the American university system, Miss Collins?" From out of somewhere a parrot-like voice gave an answer that was correct, but Cassandra was in shock. She answered the last few questions from rote. Later on, after looking at the tape no one could tell anything was wrong. She handled herself beautifully, but inside she was reeling.

Peter requested to go back stage to meet Cassandra, but when the request was handed to Cassandra, she informed the Donahue aide she would welcome the opportunity to talk with Dr. Brown, but she would rather do it at the hotel. Would he kindly meet her there for lunch?

Cassandra remained in the green room after the show and received all sorts of congratulations from the show's staff. Donahue commented on what a pleasure it was to have her on the show. Deanna was thrilled out of her mind that everything was good. Cassandra did not hear a thing she said . . . Deanna sensed something wasn't quite right.

"Are you O.K., Cassandra?"

"Yes and no. Let's get back to the hotel and I'll explain everything."

In the limousine on the way back to the hotel, Cassandra told Deanna what had transpired, not going into a great deal of detail to who Peter was and what she felt.

"Jesus Christ, you handled yourself so well you didn't miss a beat."

"Grace under pressure, huh?" they laughed and then Cassandra broke down crying.

Deanna was scared. She was afraid Cassandra was undergoing a psychotic break.

"Do you want a sedative, Cassandra?"

"No thanks, I'll be fine. Just need time to meditate and pull myself together. This has been a chance I've waited half my life to have, and I want to be clear as I can be."

Sensing Deanna's concern she said, "Don't worry about me kid, I'll be fine."

Pulling up to the hotel Cassandra put on her best public smile and left the limousine radiant, as if nothing at all had transpired

The phone in the hotel lobby rang for Cassandra. She picked it up, shaking like a bowl of Jello.

"Yes."

"Cassandra, its Peter. Where shall I meet you?"

"Why don't you come up here, Peter. I don't think we should have this conversation in public. After all its been fourteen years." Cassandra felt the silence on the other end of the line. What did it mean?

"Yes, I'm aware of that, I'll be right up." Peter's heart was pounding, his feeling was as intense for Cassandra as it ever was. Why did she never answer his letter? What happened to their baby? These were questions he would have to have answered from her own lips before he rested.

The hatred of the rejection he suffered, the weight of the years, and the great love, time left undiminished, were all swirling around in his mind. He would at last find the answers and be free. He could then live his life as a full and healthy man, no longer tormented by the demons that haunted him day and night. Cassandra held the key.

Peter went up to her suite on the top floor. He rang the bell and Deanna answered the door.

"Hello."

"Good afternoon. Dr. Peter Brown to see Miss Collins." She ushered him inside.

"How do you do? Have a seat, she will be out shortly."

"Thank you." He seated himself. Cassandra brushed her hair back and put on lip gloss. She walked out into the sitting room with her head held high.

"Hello Peter." When she looked at him, her heart began to break. The tears all the years had been unable to wash away started to gush as she collapsed into his arms.

Epilogue

Cassandra sat down at her carved oak desk and opened up the top drawer, taking out a piece of fine vellum stationery. Her name, Mrs. Peter Brown, was embossed in gold ink on the fine letterhead.

Lake Wylie, N.C.

Dear Danny,

I'm sorry I haven't written you in several weeks. I miss our morning coffees so. Things here are fine. Baby Catherine is starting to teethe, and she is gaining weight, just like her pregnant mother. I am expecting another baby this spring. I know this will the boy Peter has been praying for. I feel good, and the doctor says I am in great shape for an "old lady. I guess they will be Irish twins, thirteen months apart.

Peter's practice is thriving. He is respected here in the medical community, and he is making great inroads with his ideas on therapy using hypnosis and past life regressions.

We can't wait for you to visit us soon. Life in New York seems like a dream I had long ago. Every day I spend here with Peter and the baby makes me realize how good life is.

Love,
Cassandra